WEB OF TRAITORS

AN ADVENTURE STORY OF ANCIENT ATHENS

Web of

GEOFFREY TREASE

Author of "Cue for Treason," "Sir Walter Raleigh," etc.

Traitors

NEW YORK   THE VANGUARD PRESS, INC.

For J.
And Her Friends
Who Chose Greek

Fourth Printing

L. C. CATALOGUE CARD NUMBER: 52–11124

NOTE: This book was published in England under
the title, *The Crown of Violet*

Manufactured in the United States of America by
H. Wolff, New York, N. Y.

CONTENTS

A TRIP TO THE THEATER

1

No school today! Hurray, hurray!"

Alexis woke with a start. Anyone would, with a noisy young brother chanting that in his ear.

He sat up, the leather straps of the bedstead squeaking under him. Through sleepy, narrowed eyes—which made him look even more faunlike than usual—he saw that it was still not fully light in the yard outside. But it was light enough to see the mad gray shape of Theo capering round the room. With a yawn he groped behind him for the pillow.

"No school today!" Theo rejoiced. "Hurray, hurray, no —" The pillow caught him off his balance, and he collapsed in midsentence. He leaped up good-temperedly, his round face beaming.

"Now will you pipe down?" Alexis demanded, snuggling his bare shoulders under the purple blanket again. "And if you dare to chuck that pillow back," he added, as Theo seemed to be considering the idea, "you'll get a taste of my slipper!"

"I was only looking at it," Theo protested. "It's bust open. I'm all feathers."

"What do you expect? You *will* start crowing in the middle of the night, like a blessed cock."

"It isn't the middle of the night—the sky is perceptibly brightening," said Theo with dignity, using one of the grown-up phrases he loved to pick up and introduce into his conversation. "Do you realize what day it is?"

Alexis sat up again, this time more briskly, threw back the blanket, and swung his feet to the floor.

"My stars! The Theater Festival!"

He was now fully awake. His slanty brown eyes sparkled.

"Of course," said Theo. "Three days off school!"

"That's all you think about, lazy little object." Alexis stretched his arms. "Well, *I've* finished with school now."

Theo grinned. "That may be your idea—it's not Father's. You've got to do higher education——"

"I'll give you some lower education if you don't look out!" Alexis aimed a kick which, since he was still barefoot, he never meant to land. Theo gave a squeak of mock terror and went hurdling over his own bed and then over the empty one by the door. That was Philip's, but he, being nineteen, was doing his second year of military service on the frontier, and had not managed to get home for the Festival.

Safe in the doorway, Theo paused to bargain. "Bring my towel," he begged, "and then I'll get the water."

"Oh, all right," Alexis grumbled. He enjoyed barking at Theo, but very seldom bit. He picked up both towels and followed his brother into the yard.

All over Athens the cocks were crowing. The square of sky enclosed by the buildings had turned from dark-blue to oyster-gray, though a thin sickle moon still shone amid the branches of the fig tree.

Theo was bent over the well. Argus—they called him Argus after the faithful dog in the *Odyssey*—was nosing affectionately at his ribs. "Gerraway, Argus!" he pleaded. "Stop slobbering! Your nose is cold——"

"Come here, Argus!" Argus obediently flung himself at Alexis, and was gently repulsed. "Down, Argus! You hurt. Put some sandals on your claws—you scratch."

The bucket came up. Theo tilted it and filled a big earthenware jar. There was some water left, so he threw it playfully at the hound, who retired behind the fig tree with an injured expression, as though to say: if I am not permitted to scratch other people, does anyone object if I scratch myself?

Alexis lifted the jar and poured some water into his brother's cupped hands. Theo bent forward, splashed it into his face, rubbed and snorted for a moment, and then groped for the towel. His passion for cleanliness was quickly satisfied.

"Now you," he said.

Even at dawn, the air in the courtyard was mild. The house, standing around it on all four sides, had trapped and held the warmth of yesterday. The water, ic-cold from the dark well, took Alexis' breath away at the first shock. But, dashing the sleep from his eyes and determined to set a good example, he said between chattering teeth, "Pour the rest over my head if you like," and privately hoped there was not too much left.

"Bend down, then," said Theo cheerfully, "I'm not as tall as you—yet."

Alexis bent like a discus thrower. The water came down in a green-white arc, smelling of the earth. It shattered itself on his crinkly brown hair, splashed to his shoulders, and ran down his back till every knot in his spine glistened.

"Ooh!" he gasped. "*Aah!*"

The water gurgled down the gutter, through the entrance passage, and under the still-bolted door into the street. "Like another bucket?" Theo offered, but Alexis had fled, towel in hand, dripping and shaking himself like a dog.

By the time he had put on his tunic, a crisp new white one with a gay blue pattern zigzagging round the edge, he could hear his mother overhead, waking the maids. Out in the yard Theo was meekly pouring water over his father's hands, and white-haired Parmeno was standing respectfully at his master's elbow, holding the clean robe he would drape over his tunic before leaving the house. His mother, of course, and his sister Nico (who was seventeen and came between him and Philip) would wash in their bedrooms. Syra was just getting their jugs.

He did not like Syra, pretty though she was. "Far *too* pretty," Mother used to say darkly, "for a house slave where there are boys growing up." Syra gave herself airs and called herself a lady's maid, because she walked behind Mother in the street to carry the parcels. Thratta, the housemaid, did ten times as much work, but would have been hopeless as an escort—squint-eyed, ungainly, loud-voiced, and with a most barbarous Thracian accent. But Alexis loved her, as they all did.

He went to seek her now. "What about breakfast, Thratta darling?"

"I have no time to bother with breakfast." She did not even turn her head, but went on packing the big lunch basket. "Bread's yonder. You can dip it in yourself, can't you?"

"I might manage that." He poured a little wine into a cup and dipped a crust into it. Theo came into the kitchen.

"What's *in* the basket?" he demanded.

"You'll see when it's opened." She glanced round, seized a handful of eggs, and crammed them in. Theo cried out in alarm.

"They're hard-boiled, you idiot," Alexis reassured him.

"I can see apples and figs," Theo went on, more to himself than anyone else. "I *deduce* honey cakes, because I saw them being made last night. I hope there is cold sausage. I bet there's cheese. Any nuts, Thratta?"

"One or two, maybe."

"Good." He wagged his round head approvingly. "Nuts are *right*, at the theater."

"Don't you mean," Alexis suggested sarcastically, "that they're indispensable to the appreciation of the drama?"

Theo blinked, then smiled sweetly as he took in the beauty of the words and stored them away in his memory for future use. "Yes," he said, "absolutely."

"Well," said Thratta, contemplating the heaped-up basket. "You should have enough here. Though it beats me how any of you can eat a bite, after listenin' to all them horrors."

Never having seen a play, Thratta had rather peculiar ideas about them. She had picked up jumbled fragments of plots, mainly the more sensational episodes, such as Agamemnon's wife murdering him in his bath, Medea sending a poisoned robe to destroy the princess on her wedding day, and Prometheus chained to the crag while a vulture tore at his liver. She might have been bitterly disappointed if she had gone to the Festival and discovered that the more bloodcurdling events happened off-stage. That did not stop Theo from saying, as he always did, "Don't you wish you were coming with us, Thratta dear?"

"Theater's not for slave girls. We'll have a nice day, don't worry, once the lot of you is packed off. And now get out of my kitchen—there's your ma an' Nico in the yard."

"Everyone ready?" Father demanded.

"All present and correct, sir," Alexis assured him.

It was like a military parade when Father ran his eye over the family before an important occasion. He himself was such a distinguished figure, with his gray curly beard and lean muscular body, still as straight-backed as when he had fought in the heavy infantry—his cheek and his right forearm showed pale scars where he had been wounded. He was pointed out to strangers in the street as Leon, who had once been good enough to run in the Olympian games, and Alexis always felt a warm stab of pride when he heard them whisper, and saw their interested stare follow his father out of sight.

Then there was Mother, quiet and rather nervous, smoothing the folds of her dark-red robe, and Nico, in blue and white stripes, demure under Father's eye. Both wore veils—Father insisted on that. He was old-fashioned, fond of saying that "woman's place was in the home," and that the best reputation any girl could have was to be completely unheard-of outside the family circle. It was a wonder that Mother and Nico were allowed their theater trip at all.

This morning, however, it was the boys he inspected most keenly. First their garlands—everybody had to wear a garland of ivy leaves today, in honor of the god Dionysus, whose feast it was. Then the rest of their appearance. "Shift that clasp on your shoulder, Theopompus, it's making your cape fall badly. It should be two or more inches to the left. Remember, a cultured person can be told by the way he drapes his clothes."

"Yes, Father."

"And you, Alexis, now that you're old enough to wear a man's tunic, wear it *like* a man. Don't just put your head and arms through it and drag a belt round your middle! Straighten it. And when we're at the theater, don't let me have to be nudging you every five minutes for crossing your legs—it's an ungainly, barbarous attitude."

"No, Father."

So they got off, Father in front, stick in hand, with the boys on either side, then Mother and Nico, and Parmeno bringing up the rear with the lunch basket and an armful of cushions. Parmeno was the only one of the slaves who went to the theater, but then, Parmeno was different. His normal job was to escort the boys to school and games, stay with them, and bring them back. He could read and write fluently, and was really quite a well-educated man. So he should be, Alexis sometimes reflected, for he's spent half his life sitting at the back of classrooms, hearing the same old lessons year after year—arithmetic and music, the *Iliad* and the *Odyssey*—and if *he* can't remember them, how can they expect us boys to, who only have them from seven to sixteen?

Well, that was over now, so far as he was concerned.

From today—or rather in three days' time, when the Festival ended—a new life would begin. It would be two years before he was old enough for the army. Class lessons were behind him, he would go to lecturers and tutors. He would go to them, and to the gymnasium, alone. I'm glad Father isn't rich, he told himself for the hundredth time. If he owned more slaves, he'd have one following me around. But there's only dear old Parmeno, and he can't be in two places at once, and he'll have to stick with Theo, because he's the youngest.

Freedom . . . new things. . . .

Athenian to his finger tips, Alexis thrilled at the very suggestion of the words. Somehow, from now on, life would be so much more exciting, so much more adventurous. It *must* be.

He could not have said exactly how this was to happen.

And he would have been amazed, and more than a little shaken, if some divine oracle had told him that one adventure, greater than any he could have expected, was to start—though hidden and unnoticed like a river's source—that very day.

2

The sun had cleared the eastward ridges. It shone down the narrow streets, lighting up the whitewashed walls with their painted woodwork, their scribbled *Vote for Telys* or *Archias loves Dio*, and their daubed cartoons of political leaders. Everybody was going in the same direction.

"Come on, let's hurry," Theo nagged. "All the best seats will be taken."

Father laughed. He was in holiday mood himself now and he said nothing about dignity or deportment, only, "This isn't a marathon. Think of poor Parmeno with the basket!"

"What are the plays about this year? Who's going to win? There's a boy at school whose father's awfully rich, and it's his turn to pay for one of them, and *he* says—"

When Theo started, it was easy for others to drop out of the conversation. Alexis walked on in silence, happy enough to direct his eyes and ears and thoughts elsewhere.

15

Those people in front must be strangers, Dorians from the western islands, or even, to judge by their voices, from beyond . . . the two swarthy men with soft dark eyes, whose hands fluttered like birds as they talked, must be Egyptian merchants . . . the lordly person with the four attendants would be a foreign ambassador. . . . People from every country came to Athens during the season of the Great Dionysia.

And why not? he thought with patriotic pride.

Wasn't Athens the finest city-state in Greece—and weren't the Greeks the only fully civilized people in the world? He could not, of course, remember Pericles, who had built up Athens' glory and made her "the school of Greece." But he had heard so much from Father, who had hero-worshiped Pericles in his own youth, that he almost felt he had known the great statesman at first hand. Father said nothing had ever been the same since he died. When the news was bad, he would shake his head and growl, "It wouldn't have happened if Pericles had lived." In time it had become a family joke, something to say if you knocked over the wine jar or spilled stew down your clothes.

Athens had never looked lovelier than in that early golden sunlight. His heart swelled with the beauty of it. He wanted to run up to every foreigner, pluck him by the cloak, and ask, What do you think of our city? Isn't it a splendid place?

To reach the theater they had to walk round the Acropolis hill. Steep grassy slopes ran up to sheer cliffs of lilac-tinted marble, crowned in turn by massive walls. The road ran too close under the citadel for them to see much of the temples clustered on the summit—they could catch only a glimpse of pointed roofs, and the helmet and spear point of Athena's thirty-foot statue of flashing bronze, which sailors used as a landmark when their galleys were still miles out at sea.

But, as the road climbed the gentler slope, above the market place and the main part of the city, it became the finest thoroughfare in Athens, lined on both sides with statues and memorials to past prize winners in the Theater Festival. Now, too, there was a long view northward over the housetops and outer ramparts to the green countryside, with the river Cephisus winding under its fringe of gray poplars and brighter plane trees. Farms and villages were dotted among the small cornfields and orchards: Colonus, where there were always nightingales, and, farther away, Acharnae, where the charcoal burners lived. Beyond Acharnae ran the mountains, still dappled with the winter snows, their lower slopes dark with pine forest or lighter where the oak woods spread—Aegaleus and Parnes, and Cithaerum behind, towering to five thousand feet, shielding Athens from north winds and invaders. Somewhere up there in one of the frontier forts was poor Philip, grumbling as he polished his armor and thought of all the family going off to the theater without him.

And the family—what were they thinking about as they rounded the bend and saw the terraced seats filling the scooped-out hillside, under the south wall of the Acropolis?

"Will there be any murders?" Theo was aking Father.

"She shouldn't wear saffron yellow," Nico was telling Mother. "It doesn't go with her muddy skin."

"Won't be sorry to get rid of this basket," Parmeno was grumbling to himself behind.

Alexis was wondering what it must feel like to win the Drama Festival and be commemorated ever afterward by a victory monument in the Street of Prizes and to leave words on the lips of one's countrymen, like those of Euripides glorifying Athens:

> *Looking out on the hills olive-laden,*
> *Enchanted, where first from the earth*

The gray-gleaming fruit of the Maiden
    Athena had birth
A soft gray crown for a city
    Beloved, a City of Light . . .

Yes, to write like Euripides! That *would* be something!

Father paid, and they joined the hundreds of people streaming into the theater and clambering up the steep terraces. The front rows were kept for high officials, foreign notables, and citizens who had done something special, like winning at the Olympian games. If only Father had won his race instead of coming a close second, he would have had a place of honor there for the rest of his life. But he hadn't, so he led the way farther up, turning now and then to give Mother a hand. The high steps were awkward for long trailing dresses.

"This will do," he said at last. "Put the cushions here, Parmeno." Parmeno gladly put down his basket and arranged three cushions side by side. Father did not believe in pampering boys any more than slaves.

They had no sooner settled themselves than a tall young man, who had been standing some distance away talking to friends in another row, came bounding up the steps importantly. Father positively bristled. He was just the type of young man Father most disliked—a rich dandy, dressed up in a scarlet cloak with heavy golden fringe, high boots designed to startle, gold rings almost to his manicured nails, and (horror of horrors) long hair in the Spartan style.

Alexis nudged Theo, eager to watch Father's reactions. To his surprise the man stopped at the end of their row and said shrilly, "This is *my* seat. You'll have to move."

That was no way to tackle Father. Most courteous of men, he would not stand rudeness in other people. He looked up, and answered quietly, "You were addressing me, sir?"

"Yes, I was. You'll have to move. I'm sitting here."

An overpowering perfume was wafted along the row. He was chewing some kind of highly scented gum, and the whole family became aware of it when he opened his lips. Father eyed him severely. "Young man," he said, "I presume from your speech you are an Athenian citizen— though your hair style suggests Sparta and your magnificence is somewhat Persian——"

"Of course I'm an Athenian!"

"Then it's time you realized Athens is a democracy. Apart from the reserved seats down there, the places are open to all."

"I was here first! I only went to speak to someone. Are you going to clear out or not?"

"I am not." Father glanced round. The rows above were filling fast. "There is a perfectly good place for you a little way behind. To get six seats together would mean my wife climbing to the very top of the theater. You should have left a cushion or something."

"That's right," said a man. "He should have left something."

"Who does he think he is?" demanded several voices.

More and more people joined in. The young man colored to the roots of his elegant hair. His haughty complaints were drowned by a chorus of invitations to sit down (elsewhere), to shut up, or to take himself off to Sparta. At last, when a cry from the herald announced that the proceedings were about to start with the usual sacrifice to Dionysus, he accepted defeat and, with a flounce of his gold-fringed cloak, moved to a vacant seat behind.

"Who was he, Father?" Nico demanded in a hoarse whisper.

Father snorted. "His name's Hippias. One of the old aristocratic families. I know the type. Too much money, and nothing to do but spend it on race horses. If Pericles had lived——"

"Sh!" hissed Mother.

The priest was moving forward from his place of honor in the front row. The offering was made. For a few moments twelve thousand people stood in worship of the god. Then, as they sank back on the benches, the herald's voice pealed out, clear as a trumpet: "Euripides, son of Mnesarchus, presents his tragedy—"

Down the spine of Alexis ran a delicious shiver of excitement as the play began.

For the rest of the morning Alexis was far away in space and time. He forgot the hard bench and the people around him. The real world rising behind the stage building was blotted out: he saw neither the great mauve mass of Hymettus ridge, nor the bright white shingle down at Phalerum, nor the blue gulf beyond, specked with sails. Even when a sea gull flashed low over the theater he scarcely noticed.

The high narrow stage and the circular dancing space in front had become the whole world. The actors, towering to more than natural size with their high headdresses and masks, their thick-soled boots and padded robes, *were* the gods and goddesses, the bygone heroes and heroines whose stories he had learned at school. The music helped to cast the spell—the flute, now sad and plaintive, now wildly emotional, and the choruses, chanted by the dancing men as they moved to and fro, weaving their patterns of stately movement between the episodes of the play. But chiefly it was the poetry, sometimes declaimed in a long passionate

speech or a thoughtful soliloquy, sometimes tossed to and
fro, like a ball, in crisp, single lines of dialogue.

He had always loved poetry at school—Homer's long stories and the brief lyrics that caught a flash of beauty, a
joke, or a thought in a dozen lines—but most of all he
loved the poetry of the theater. That was what he loved to
learn by heart and sometimes tried to make up—secretly,
confessing to nobody but his best friend. It was easy
enough to make up a straightforward blank-verse speech,
but the lyric choruses, with their elaborate meters and patterns, one part having to match another part exactly, syllable for syllable, took some doing.

Yet how superbly Euripides did it, without any apparent
effort, so that listening you never thought of meter, never
even thought of the lines as having been planned and con-
structed and written down months before! They poured
from the speakers' lips as though they had sprung straight
from their hearts.

Under the Festival rules Euripides had entered a group
of three tragedies. They lasted until noon, and it was only
then that Alexis came out of his trance.

"Wasn't that grand?" said Theo. "But I wish they'd
done the killing on the stage so we could see it, instead of
just drawing back the curtains and showing the bodies
when it was all over."

"You *are* a little barbarian. It would be very bad taste."

"I don't see why."

"Murder—killing people at all—must be horribly ugly.
No Greek would make a show of it in the theater. Some
things," added Alexis loftily, "are best left to the imagination."

Theo was disposed to argue the point, but luckily Parmeno opened the lunch basket. There was a cold chicken
as well as the sausage, hard-boiled eggs, and cheese; gleam-

ing apples, sugary figs and raisins, crunchy honey cakes, wine, and water to mix with it, and enough nuts to keep their jaws busy halfway through the afternoon performance. No wonder Parmeno's arm had ached.

When at last even Theo had eaten all he could, he licked his fingers, gave a sigh of contentment, and said, "Now it's the comedies! Hurray!"

Parmeno was packing the empty jars into the basket. Mother and Nico stood up, brushing crumbs from their dresses, Nico with a rather rebellious expression. Theo promptly grabbed her cushion, sat on it, and grinned up at her unsympathetically.

"Hard luck, Nico! Don't you wish you could stay?"

Nico shrugged her shoulders but no retort slipped through her pouting lips. Mother said quickly,

"Certainly not! The comedies are not for ladies."

"Why not?" Theo persisted wickedly.

"Because," broke in Father firmly, "they deal with current affairs, not old legends, and as ladies know nothing about politics, they would only be bored."

"Would you be bored, Nico?"

His sister tossed her dark, garlanded head. "How can I tell," she said shortly, "unless I'm allowed to try?"

"Well, you certainly won't be," said Father.

"Oh, dear no," said Mother in a flutter. "It isn't only the politics. Many of the jokes are—well, extremely rude."

"I think, my dear," said Father, "you had better be going now—most of the other ladies have gone and it must be nearly time for the comedies to start. Come back and meet us at the end of the afternoon, Parmeno."

They went, and the diminished audience spread itself at ease along the rows. "It doesn't seem fair," Alexis muttered to himself. It was the first time he had spoken during the argument.

There were two comedies. The first, though it amused Theo, was a feeble affair, and the audience did not trouble to hide its opinion. People whistled and clucked with their tongues, and toward the end those sitting near enough sent showers of nutshells and squashed fruit raining onto the stage. It was all the actors could do to finish the play.

"How awful for them," said Alexis, "*and* the author—I wonder how he's feeling?"

"If they put on rubbish," said Father, "they can't blame people for criticizing. Free speech, that's the Athenian way."

The second comedy was much better. It was by Aristophanes, who had been writing for ages and had several times won the prize. It was a rollicking piece, with a fantastic farcical plot, absurd characters, and ridiculous situations which made Alexis rock with laughter, the tears running down his cheeks. The script was a wonderful mixture: there were jokes of extreme subtlety, digs at politicians, take-offs of famous public figures, parodies of lines in tragedies, puns, tongue twisters, allusions he could not always understand; there were other jokes as broad and vulgar as any he had heard whispered round the class at school; and there were choruses as beautiful in their poetry as any heard that morning.

The audience loved it all. But most they loved the interlude in the middle, when the leader of the chorus stepped forward and spoke directly to them in a long speech of lilting verse, neatly running over the topics of the day with special reference to certain well-known personages. At every other line the audience clapped and roared with delight.

"Say," Theo whispered in awe, after a particularly bold thrust at the expense of one politician, "I don't know how he *dares*."

" 'Free speech, that's the Athenian way,' " Alexis solemnly mimicked Father under his breath. Theo gurgled appreciatively, but with a cautious sidelong glance at Father, who was chuckling with delight—but at the play.

It ended, all too soon, with a wild banquet on the stage, men dressed up as dancing girls, and a mock wedding procession. As the chorus marched off there was prolonged applause.

Theo jumped up, rubbing his stiff joints. "Wasn't that *marvelous*, Father? The other comedies will have to be pretty good, the next two days, to beat that."

Alexis stood up also, his brown eyes dancing with fun and excitement. He was drunk with plays and poetry, as a man might be with wine. A few lines of verse had formed themselves, almost ready-made, in his own mind. They were not very witty, but they tickled his fancy and before he could stop to think he grabbed Theo's arm and said, "I think I shall write a comedy—how would this sound?" Striking an attitude, with a flounce of an imaginary cloak, he declaimed in the affected tone of a young aristocrat: *"Know you not who I am? I'm Hippias!"* Then, changing character, he answered himself: *"From your long locks I thought you were a lass."* Theo, who was easily amused, burst out laughing and Alexis, thus encouraged, went on with his performance.

"Where is my seat? Why must it be behind?" A fourth line underlined the double meaning in an obvious way which set Theo chortling with glee. Suddenly, and too late, Alexis realized that he had a larger audience.

Hippias was standing only a few yards away, his pale features twitching with fury. His was the face of a man slow to forgive anything, but least of all being made to look a fool. Alexis knew in that instant he had made an enemy. How dangerous an enemy, he had yet to learn.

3

Life seemed flat after three days of Theater Festival and the excitement of the last evening when the winners were announced and people held parties all over the city.

Theo went off to school as usual. Alexis and his father called on Milon, the teacher of public speaking who was to give Alexis lessons. But this morning he was suffering from a severe headache ("too much celebrating last night," Alexis murmured), and he sent his apologies by the door-keeper. He was seeing no pupils today. Classes would resume tomorrow.

Alexis was not sorry.

This was a question—and not the only question—on which he and his father did not see eye to eye. He had said, weeks ago, "But, Father, I don't *want* to make public speeches."

"You don't know yet," said Father, reasonably enough. "You're only a boy. When you grow up, you'll take your place in the Assembly. Then there's lawsuits. You may not want to go to law, but somebody may bring an action against you—Athens is full of quarrelsome busybodies. You'll have to defend yourself. Nobody can do it for you. And with a jury maybe of five hundred it'll be no good mumbling in the depths of your beard."

This danger seemed to Alexis rather remote. So far he had only the faintest down on his upper lip. But it was no use answering Father with a frivolous point like that. Instead, he had seized on the really weak part of his argument.

"But *you* never speak in the Assembly!"

"No, I don't——"

"Then why should I?"

Then Father had said a surprising thing. Surprising, because he never paid his sons compliments, Alexis least of all. "Because, lad, you've got the brains of the family."

"*I* have? But——"

"Oh, yes. You'll never make an athlete like your brother Philip, let alone young Theopompus. . . . *He's* going to be good, if he goes on like this—only don't tell him so. . . ."

Father's face had softened. There were thoughts behind his eyes, and Alexis found he could read them. Father's real ambition was to have sons competing at Olympia as he had done—sons who perhaps would win, as he had not, and be welcomed home to Athens as public heroes, honored for the rest of their lives. What a disappointment *I* must have been, he thought sadly, remembering his own merely average performances on the sports field.

"You'll never win any laurels that way," Father went on, "but you may do something nearly as good—just as good, I should say. You've got your wits about you. You've the gift of gab. You can make us all laugh with that quick tongue of yours. And, young as you are, you follow all the news."

"Yes, but——"

"Your way is clear. I should be very proud to have a son who spoke in the Assembly. The country needs some decent men in politics, to get us on our feet again."

So it had been decided that he should go to Milon's classes in the art of oratory, and learn to express himself effectively in words. Privately, he thought that there might be better ways of doing that than by making long speeches in the Assembly, but for the time being he must obey without argument. Just the same, he was delighted when the doorkeeper brought out the message that, owing to a slight indisposition, the learned professor would be unable to take his classes that day.

"What will you do now?" asked Father. He was anxious to get down to the potteries, to make sure that the slaves had started work and were not just gossiping after the holidays.

"Oh . . ." Alexis hesitated. "I suppose I'll go round for Lucian. We might get up a game of hockey, or go for a walk."

Father nodded. He approved of Lucian. Lucian was good-looking without being girlish, first-rate at all sports, and born of a respectable family, neither risen from the gutter nor claiming some fancy pedigree from the gods. Altogether, he was what Father called "a healthy influence."

"If you do go for a walk," he said, "you might take a message to the farm. Say I shall be coming out to look at things in a day or two, and I want to see the place shipshape."

"All right, Father, I'll do that."

Half an hour later the two boys were walking through the city gates along the eastern road. It was about four miles to the little farm which Father, like so many businessmen, owned as well as his town house. Alexis loved the farm, nestling white amid the green foothills, with its shimmering gray olive trees and terraced vines, its hovering bees and skirmishing hens, the piglets and the old donkey and the two cows with their big, mild eyes.

They delivered their message to the peasant couple who looked after the place, rested awhile in the shade drinking milk, and then set off again.

"Let's explore up the river," Lucian suggested.

"Yes, let's. We might have a swim."

They struck off, through the orchards, to where the Ilissus came tumbling down through its steep little valley from the slopes of Hymettus and Pentelicus.

Lucian was the taller by a couple of inches, dark-haired, olive-skinned, sleek and graceful as a thoroughbred. Alexis, stockier, brown, and curly, skipped beside him like a goat.

Years ago they had vowed eternal friendship, like the famous pairs of ancient times, like Achilles and Patroclus in the *Iliad*. Alexis had always thought himself lucky to be singled out as Lucian's best friend, because Lucian could have had anyone. Other boys swarmed round him like bees. "The thing about you," Lucian had once confessed to Alexis "is that you never ran after me and got tiresome. And you often make me laugh."

A cuckoo called from the oak wood. Violets flecked the thin turf of the hillside. They came out, round Athens, in early December, and you could pick them as late as the middle of May.

"Plenty of water coming down still," said Lucian.

By midsummer the Ilissus would be nearly dried up, a series of shrinking pools connected by stretches of clean white boulders. But so far it was still drawing on the snows of last winter and the rains of spring. There were rapids of fluffy foam, and smooth curves of water falling over rock ledges like long green manes of hair. Below these cataracts were calm pools, translucent, every pebble on the bottom distinct.

In one such pool they swam. It was sharply cold, because the sun was filtered through the mesh of overhanging leaves. Where the pool did catch the sunbeams it reflected them in strange, rainbow-tinted blobs of light, wavering on the shadowy gray rock face above. Alexis could have watched them for minutes together.

Lucian splashed him, wallowing in the pool like a dolphin. "Wake up, Alex! Or have you turned to stone?"

They played about for awhile, then climbed out to dry in the full sunshine which poured down upon a shelf above the pool. Glistening wet, they looked like statues, Alexis bronze and Lucian ivory.

"Wish we had some olive oil," Lucian grumbled.

Alexis laughed. "You'll have to start carrying an oil flask."

"I'm not such a snob. I leave that to the young dandies. Like that fellow Hippias." Lucian snorted contemptuously. Carrying an oil flask went with long hair, scent, and jewelry. It was the mark of the Best Families, as they regarded themselves. Other Athenians described them in less flattering terms. "Tell me again," said Lucian, "what you made up about him."

Alexis repeated the lines. He went on to make up a few more on the spot. Lucian chuckled admiringly.

"Very neat!"

"Oh, it's quite easy. It just flows out, when you're in the mood. I wish I could write *real* poetry."

"Like Homer?"

"Heavens, no! Nobody could write like Homer nowadays."

"Who, then?"

"Euripides."

Lucian looked startled. "My father doesn't approve of Euripides. He calls him 'that awful man.' They say his mother was just a common woman in the market, selling vegetables, and he divorced his wife, and——"

"That's only gossip." Sometimes Alexis found his friend a shade irritating. Lucian never questioned things, he was too conventional. "Anyhow, I can't see how it makes any difference to his plays."

"Father doesn't like his plays either. He says they put too many ideas into people's heads."

"I should have thought that was a very good thing."

"Oh, you know what I *mean*. I'm not going to argue," said Lucian, rolling over to dry the last beads of moisture from his shoulder blades, "because whatever I say, you can always turn it round somehow. But my father knows what he's talking about, and he's a little older than you."

"In that case Euripides should be the wisest of us all," said Alexis with a twinkle in his brown eyes, "because he's seventy if he's a day."

Freshened by their swim, they put on their tunics again and went farther up the gorge, carrying their sandals so that they could splash through the shallow places when it suited them.

"I like it up here," said Alexis, "miles away from everywhere and everyone."

"What was that?" Lucian stopped abruptly, his right hand clutching a slender tree trunk for support, his feet splayed on a slant of sun-baked rock.

Alexis could hear nothing but the gush and gurgle of the river in its cleft. "Was it that cuckoo again?"

"No. It was music."

"Music up here?"

"I thought so. Sort of flute. But it couldn't be, surely?"

"Not unless it was Pan himself! There aren't any mortal

shepherds around here." Alexis spoke lightly. Lucian looked nervous.

"You don't want to say things like that, Alex."

"But no one *does* graze sheep or goats just here——"

"I didn't mean that. You shouldn't mention a god's name —not in that tone. Anything might happen."

Alexis grinned. "Well, I've never heard of Pan coming as near Athens as this. It would be interesting to see him."

"Oh, shut up!" Lucian begged him. "It doesn't *do* to see one of the gods."

"Ever know anyone who did?"

"No. But there *have* been plenty of cases in the past."

"The very dim and distant past," Alexis admitted. "In fact, the poets would be hard up without them! What was this music like?"

"Oh, it was—weird. Not like any I've ever heard."

"Anyhow, doesn't your father disapprove of the flute?" said Alexis slyly.

"Yes."

"So does mine. Won't let me have lessons. 'The lyre is a gentleman's instrument,'" he mimicked, "'but the flute is too womanish and emotional.'"

"Just what my father says!"

"They're all alike," sighed Alexis. "Where do they get these ready-made opinions, all so beautifully the same? Are they dished out to registered citizens with their voting tablets?"

"I can't hear anything now," said Lucian stiffly. "Perhaps it was my imagination."

"Perhaps it was."

"Should we go on?"

"I think so. Unless you are really afraid of meeting a Certain Person, and being driven mad—or madder?"

Lucian tossed his head disdainfully, and they went on. They kept as close to the river as they could, but sometimes, when the rocks rose sheer on either side of a waterfall, they had to scramble up into the woods and work their way round. They were doing this and had just come out on a steep bluff, high above the river where it was almost invisible beneath its overarching trees, when Lucian stopped again.

"What's up now? What have you heard this time?"

"Nothing. But I saw something."

"What?"

"It looked like a head———"

"No body attached? How unpleasant!"

"Don't be a *fool*, Alex! I'm serious. It was like a white gleam down there, between the leaves———"

"Water, obviously."

"No, I'll swear it was a face, and an arm———"

"White, though? And a Certain Person is always supposed to be as brown as a berry—and hairy as a goat! Did you see any horns?"

"I wish you wouldn't talk like that," retorted Lucian. They were both talking in whispers, just in case. "Don't you believe in anything? Don't you believe in nymphs?"

"The trouble with you is Dramatic Indigestion."

"What's that?"

"Too many plays this week, all full of gods and spirits! You've got so that you're seeing them—you're suffering from Legendary Liver———"

"Listen!" said Lucian crossly. "There *are* spirits who haunt rivers. If this wasn't one, what was it? No ordinary girl would wander about up here."

"Of course not," Alexis agreed. He thought of Nico, scarcely allowed out of the house by herself. There were girls in Athens less strictly brought up—poorer girls who had to work, do the shopping, and fetch water from the public fountains—but that type would hardly set foot outside the gates.

"Then——?"

"I told you, it's imagination."

"Is *that* imagination?" Lucian demanded suddenly in a voice that was at once shaky and triumphant.

This time Alexis heard the music. It was eerie, haunting music, bubbling up from the leafy chasm below them. It beckoned him. At the same time it sent a queer thrill through his body. He felt it in his stomach. His lips were dry, but the palms of his hands grew moist.

"I've had enough of this," said Lucian. "Let's get back."

"No."

"You're not going down?" Lucian seized his wrist.

"Let go. I want to see."

"You're crazy! If it *is* a nymph, you may be changed into something—"

Alexis wrenched himself free and started down the steep cliff. In a sense Lucian's warning came true. He was never quite the same after that moment.

Lucian stood for a few seconds, fear fighting with loyalty inside him. Then, because Alexis was his best friend, he forced himself to go down, under the trees, where Alexis had just disappeared.

4

The wild music stopped suddenly as Alexis pushed aside the oleander branches at the water's edge. The nymph raised her eyes to meet his across the pool. She gave a little scream and leaped up. It was a most unnymphlike scream, verging almost upon a squawk, like the noise Nico made when Theo dropped a lizard down her back. Hearing it, Alexis was no longer afraid.

"Sorry if I scared you," he called politely.

"Oh—that's all right—" she gasped. She had been poised to run, but now she relaxed. Several yards of deep clear water divided them. She laughed unsteadily. "It was so sudden, I thought for a moment you weren't human——"

"Thanks!"

"I meant it as a compliment. You're so brown—and it was something about your eyes, I suppose——"

"I have no horns," he assured her with a smile, "and look, quite ordinary feet—no hoofs." He came out of the oleanders and stood balanced on the rim of the pool, so that she

34

could see he was just a boy in a white tunic edged with blue,
dangling rope sandals in one hand.

Lucian joined him. The girl's eyes opened wider. They
were calm, gray-blue eyes. "Any more of you?" She spoke
easily and confidently, now that she had recovered from
her first alarm, without the shy lowered tone and downcast
look of the few girls they knew. Her voice was not unmusi-
cal in itself, but her broad Doric accent grated on their
Athenian ears.

"Just us," said Alexis. "No reason to be afraid."

She had a trick of laughing silently. It was more than the
slow smile which crept over her lips at other times. "I'm not
afraid," she said coolly. "You can't get across without swimming—and by the time you were halfway over, there'd be
no me on this side. You wouldn't find me, either."

"Lucian maintained you were a nymph all along!"

"And I took *you* for Pan. How funny!"

She sat down again and began to comb out her dark hair,
which shone damply as though she had just been swimming.
She was wearing a shortish dress the color of green apples,
not very new and not improved by her recent passage
through the woods.

"We ought to be getting back," Lucian muttered. "It's
getting late. I'm hungry——"

"Hungry? Poor boy!" Her voice pealed out mockingly.
"Have some figs—catch!" There was a plop as something
fell short and sank into the depths of the river. "Oh, darn,
that was my fault! I have plenty more, only perhaps I'd
better not take a chance throwing 'em. Come over if you
want. I wasn't telling you the strict truth just now—there
is quite an easy way across, over those rocks up there."

Very soon they were sitting beside her, gratefully chewing figs. Alexis judged her to be about their own age, certainly not older. She was slender, with small, fine features
which hardly went with her rough, homely way of talking.

Her name was Corinna, and she had only just come to live in Athens. Before that, she seemed to have been traveling about. She had lived in Sicily, at Syracuse, and at Massilia in Gaul before that.

"But Mom always wanted to come back," she said.

"Back?" Alexis seized on the word. "But you're not Athenians?"

"Oh, no. Heaven knows what we are! I was born in Athens, but we moved when I was a baby."

"They're resident aliens," said Lucian, "obviously."

"Still," said Alexis, ignoring him, "I'll bet you were thrilled to come to Athens."

"Not when I got here," said the surprising girl. "I loathe the place."

"*What?*" Both boys sat up and surveyed her with goggle-eyed horror. Loathe Athens? It was a wonder the earth did not open and engulf her.

"I've seen a few towns, and I can tell you, Athens smells worse than any of 'em. Narrow, dirty streets, twisting here, there, and everywhere like a blessed maze! Now Piraeus is all right—the streets are wide and laid out so nicely——"

"Like the bars of a gridiron!" snorted Alexis. "Oh, Piraeus is very fine and modern—incidentally Athens planned and built it—but it's only our seaport. It isn't historical and holy, like the city itself."

"Have you been up on the Acropolis?" Lucian demanded.

"Not yet. Mom was going to take me. Then she was busy. And I don't think she really liked the idea of all those steps."

"You go up the Acropolis," Alexis ordered her. "There isn't a temple in Greece to touch the Parthenon."

"And there's a statue of Athena inside," said Lucian, "even bigger than the bronze one outside——"

"Forty feet high!" agreed Alexis.

"Her robes are pure gold——"

"Her face and arms are inlaid with ivory——"

"I'd love to see her," Corinna assured them. "I really will go, whether Mom takes me or not. But that's another thing I hate about Athens——"

"What?" asked Alexis, eager to defend his beloved city.

"Girls don't seem to have any freedom."

"Freedom?" Lucian echoed, scandalized. "For girls?"

"Why not?" retorted Corinna calmly. "Girls in other Greek cities have a much better time. Sport, now——"

"I hope you're not a pro-Spartan," said Lucian.

She looked at him scornfully. "Do you imagine it's only Spartan girls who go in for sport? The Argive girls do—and in Chios they even wrestle——"

"Do *you* want to wrestle?" Alexis inquired, raising his eyebrows comically. Corinna did not fit into his mental picture of brawny bulky females heaving each other out of the ring.

"No. Sport isn't everything. But in other cities women aren't shut up at home—they take an interest in everything, they even write poetry if they want to—and men talk to them, and treat them as sensible human beings!"

Lucian looked down his handsome nose. "There are some like that in Athens," he admitted, "but not *ladies*. Not Athenians either—resident aliens. So of course no Athenian could possibly marry one, even if he wanted to, because the law won't let a man marry a foreigner. My father says——"

"Speaking of fathers," Alexis cut in deftly, not wanting to hear any more of Lucian's father, whose opinions he could pretty well guess from those of his own, "what does *your* father say to your wandering about in the country by yourself? If my sister did such a thing——"

"I haven't a father. I think he died when I was a baby. Mom keeps an inn—she's a wonderful cook. We've taken that inn just off the market place, where the road turns up to the Acropolis."

"Oh, I know. I live near there."

There was a brief, awkward silence. That Corinna was no well-bred little Athenian miss had been painfully clear from the start. But—the daughter of an inn landlady! That was going a bit far. Inns were disreputable places, avoided by decent people. To live in one, to have a mother who kept one . . . Lucian looked down his nose again and said nothing.

"I don't much like it," said Corinna frankly. "I slip away when I can. Mom's pretty easygoing—she has fits of strictness and tries to make me behave, but she's too busy mostly. I come up here a lot. I've got a den. Like to see it?"

"Please," said Alexis.

"Swear a solemn oath then—swear by Earth and Sea— that you won't tell anyone."

They took the oath. To judge from Lucian's expression she need not have troubled him. He looked most unlikely to tell anyone about meeting her at all. She turned and ran softly up the slanting rock into the thicket. She was there one moment and the next she was gone. The green of her dress merged into the foliage. The gleam of face and arm was confused with the whiteness of shiny leaves catching the sunlight.

"This way!" she called, and they plunged after her. "Come on!" she called when they hesitated.

So she led them, by a short scrambling climb, into a bowl-shaped hollow in the hillside. One glance told Alexis that it was not made by Nature. The towering cliff face which enclosed it on three sides had been cut by men, though so many years ago that the bushes had sprung up thickly everywhere. It was an old quarry. The marble showed through the thin red soil—a mauve-tinted marble like that of the Acropolis hill, which had earned Athens her favorite nickname, "the city of the violet crown."

Corinna led them across the floor of the quarry. It was a jungle of lilacs in flower, and of oleanders which would soon be bursting out with blossom, white and pink and red. Water came splashing down the cliff, a slender crystal thread. Suddenly she vanished again. They stumbled on for a few paces, then stopped, parting the branches and peering in all directions. A few notes on the flute, clear, cold, and mocking, caused them to spin round and stare upward at the quarry face.

"Here," she called. "Put your feet in the fork of that tree —it's as easy as going upstairs."

Even Lucian, scrambling up last, had to admit that her den was a cunning place. It was a narrow cleft in the rock, raised about six feet above the floor of the quarry, but hidden by the upper branches of a lilac. As they stood there, jammed tight in the cleft and panting a little, they had a glimpse of great distances between the swaying masses of blossom—the green plain and the white city, and the sea far beyond.

"It's a tight squeeze here," said Corinna, "but then, I've never done any entertaining before." She slipped back into the shadowy cleft. "It widens out behind. A regular cave."

"Say," said Alexis admiringly. "I see now why you were so sure you could have given us the slip if you'd wanted to. We'd never have tracked you here."

"It goes a long way back," said Lucian. "It would be fun to bring torches and see how far it goes."

"I wouldn't," she advised him. "I have a little lamp I keep here—only I think I've used up all the oil. Once I did go quite far in, but it didn't look safe."

"Safe?"

"There's been one fall of rock. I'd hate there to be another when you were underneath."

"So would Lucian," said Alexis. "Personally, I'm more

than satisfied with your entrance hall. It's not so stuffy, and the sea view, though somewhat restricted, is quite charming."

She gave one of her almost-silent laughs. "You do talk funny, Alexis. I like it."

"I'll teach you to talk funny, if you like," he offered gravely. "By which I mean good Athenian—the purest Greek there is."

She tossed her head. "I don't know if I want to. Now, if you'd teach me to read and write better——"

"Can't you? No, I suppose if your mother is—well, so busy——"

"I've picked up quite a lot, I can do letters and accounts, but I wish I could read books."

"I'll help you," he promised, "on one condition."

"What's that?" Her frank eyes narrowed.

"That you teach me to play the flute."

"I'll do my best."

"I've always wanted to. It's rather looked down on with us, you know. It's all right at the theater, and it's all right for professionals to play at parties, but it's not the thing for a gentleman. The music's too wild, and you make such undignified faces when you blow into it."

"How silly!"

"Say," interrupted Lucian urgently. "It's getting terribly late. We ought to be starting back."

Alexis looked at Corinna. "Are you coming?"

"No, I'll stay up here a little longer. I want to keep out of the way till bedtime. Don't worry about me."

"All right." Lucian had already dropped to the ground. Alexis swung himself into a tree. "Don't forget you're going to teach me the flute sometime."

As they trudged home in the lengthening shadows of the poplars, Lucian said, "Of course you were joking? It might

be fun to go back some day, if we were sure she wasn't there
—but you couldn't possibly want to see her again."

"Why not?"

"But, Alex—a girl like that, a foreigner, living at a low
inn! I thought she was *awful*. Just a common little thing.
I never expected for a moment—"

Nor had Lucian expected for a moment the loud slap
which now landed on his cheek, reddening the rose already
so much admired by those who appreciated his youthful
beauty. An instant later, the partners in eternal friendship
were struggling ferociously in the dust.

5

Say you're sorry!" panted Lucian, squatting astride his friend.

Alexis ceased to squirm and heave. The brief rough-and-tumble had helped him to work off his anger, and his normal sense of humor was beginning to return. "I'm extremely sorry—" he jerked out, "sorry you're sitting on my stomach——"

"I don't mean that, I mean sorry you hit me."

"Well, as that was the cause which led to the effect," said Alexis, reasoning like a philosopher, "it follows that if I am sorry about the effect I must, logically, be——"

"Oh, dry up. I believe you could argue in *any* position. Are you sorry you slapped my face? Yes or no?"

"Well, on one hand——"

"Yes or no," insisted Lucian. "I think I'll practice for the torch ride." They were both taking part in a boys' mounted relay race in a few days' time. Lucian's idea of practicing was to go through the motions of riding on his friend's

42

stomach, bringing down his full weight at regular and fre-
quent intervals, and squashing most of the breath out of
Alexis at each impact.

"Y-y-yes!" Alexis managed to gasp at the third attempt.
Lucian dismounted, and they both scrambled to their feet.
"Mind you," said Alexis, "that proves nothing whatever, ex-
cept that you're bigger than I am. Which we knew before."

Lucian wisely said no more about Corinna herself. But,
as they trudged on into the sunset, he made clear what he
thought about girls in general. "Of course, a man's got to
marry and have a family sooner or later, but females are a
sheer waste of time till then. My father says that thirty is
the ideal age to marry, and till then a fellow's got plenty
of other things to think about—games, and the army, and
friends. He says friendship's the biggest thing in life. You
can't be *friends* with the opposite sex, he says—they can't
hold an intelligent conversation—"

Remembering Corinna, Alexis wondered. "Oh, no," he
murmured with an irony so gentle that Lucian seemed un-
aware of it.

Lucian went on talking, and he went on muttering non-
committal answers, and they both went on walking. The
sun, almost horizontal in their faces, filled the whole western
sky with golden glory, and against it the Acropolis loomed
as a mass of purple shadow, resting on the rooftops of the
town.

Lucian's father might be right, that friendship was the
biggest thing in life. Most Athenians, man and boy, would
have agreed with him. But Lucian's friendship with Alexis
had taken a sharper knock than either cared to admit.

Matters were not improved by the torch ride. It was rather
a novelty, at least for young riders. Relay races with torches
were an old-established custom, but it was only a year or two
since somebody had had the bright idea of holding a point·

to-point horse race on similar lines. After that it was merely
a question of time before the boys, who already had their
own foot races, clamored to imitate the men in this as well.

The boys' torch ride was to be the main item in the evening program of Poseidon's Festival. This was most fitting
because everyone knew that Poseidon, besides being the god
of the sea, had created the horse as a gift to mankind. It was
he who had taught men the use of the bridle, and, at some
misty date in the remote past, had instituted the very first
horse race.

There were ten teams, as usual, one from each division
making up the citizens' register. Both boys were riding for
the Leontis team. This was not such an honor as it sounded,
because the whole event was an experiment and nearly all
the young riders were of unknown quality. It was partly a
question of who could get horses, since very few people
owned them. Lucian had a well-to-do uncle with a couple of
mounts to lend, and it had been easy for Lucian to get himself and his friend included among the eight who were to
carry the torch for Leontis.

"Lightning really does live up to her name," he told
Alexis. "She's a real flier. Uncle imported her from Thessaly
—they know how to breed horses there. Though Star can
move too."

"I liked Star that day we tried them."

"Still, I really meant you to have Lightning. But Uncle
thought as I was used to her and heavier than you——"

"Of course. Mighty good of him to trust me on Star."

"I knew you'd understand. Look, Alex, it's tricky passing
those torches. We ought to practice. We can have the
horses any evening—how about it?"

Lucian was so eager, Alexis did not like to say no. It was
pleasant enough, riding in the cool of the day. He liked the
short, exhilarating gallop up to the change-over point, and
the exciting moment when they rode knee to knee, passing

a stick from hand to hand. But it took time, and his days were full now.

Every morning he had to spend hours with Milon, the professor of public speaking. That meant grammar and logic, voice production and gesture. It meant stuffing his mind with useful quotations and clever allusions, and learning to persuade people by the arguments which would most appeal to them, whether those arguments were right or wrong. "Remember always to whom you are speaking," Milon would remind his pupils with a sly smile. "Say one thing to an audience of rich men, another thing to the poor. Arguments which appeal to the young may not be the best to put before old people—and vice versa." Alexis enjoyed an argument as much as anybody, but all this seemed artificial and dishonest. He had no ambitions to shine as a public speaker anyhow, but he continued to attend Milon's classes obediently and to prepare the exercises expected of him. As he also had to spend the first part of the afternoon in the gymnasium or on the sports field he had now hardly a moment to himself, to read or to write down the scraps of poetry which often came floating into his head. So, walking back at sunset after their third rehearsal, he said, "If you don't mind, Lucian, I'll skip tomorrow."

"But it's only three days to the race!"

"I know. But one more practice should do."

"Seems a pity to miss the chance," Lucian grumbled. "After all, it's practice makes perfect."

"Too much makes you stale. You get bored——"

"I'm sorry if you were bored."

"I was thinking of the horses," said Alexis truthfully. "They've got the hang of it now, and I don't think they see the fun in doing the same thing over and over again. I've loved it, but I simply *must* have some time for other things."

"What things?" Lucian's tone was so vexed that Alexis hesitated before replying. Lucian misunderstood his hesitation. "You needn't tell me—I can guess! That girl we met—"

Alexis stared. It was not true to say that he had never thought of Corinna since that afternoon. He had, more than once. He liked her, was amused by her, and was interested in her unusual, un-Athenian point of view. He had kept his eyes open for her when passing near her mother's inn and the public fountain where the women of that district clustered if they had no water supply in their own homes. But he had neither seen her again nor formed any plan to do so. The days had been far too full.

A little while ago he would have told Lucian the simple truth: that he had been able to borrow a copy of the play, *Medea,* and wanted to enjoy it in a quiet corner away from everybody, and that afterward he wanted to try his hand at writing a chorus in the style of Euripides. He would not have confessed that last ambition to anyone but his best friend. And now, meeting the distrust in Lucian's eyes, he was too proud to tell even him.

"Can't I have an hour to myself without accounting for it to you?"

"Oh, as many as you like! I'll see you at the torch race."

So there were no more practices, and, though they saw each other every afternoon at games, Lucian always managed to surround himself with a group of other boys.

Alexis found himself with three spare evenings, and did not enjoy them as much as he had expected. He read *Medea* twice and learned the bits he liked best; then he started to write a tragedy himself, about Patroclus and Achilles. Into this he poured some of his own churned-up feelings, which was a relief, but not much. Then came the race.

The course was roughly diamond-shaped. It started from a small shrine of Poseidon, near the beach at Phalerum Bay, ran almost due north to the Long Walls linking the

city with Piraeus, and then swung west to the Itonian
Gate, the turning point. Here Alexis, riding Number Five,
would take over the torch and carry it down the Phalerum
road. After about five furlongs he would pass it over to
Lucian, and two older boys would cover the last stages
back to the sea-god's shrine.

The race was to start just after sunset, when the torches
would show up well but it would not be so dark as to make
galloping dangerous. Some of the more enthusiastic spectators—the horse fanciers, the parents and best friends of the
various competitors—strolled out to line the course or to
see the start and finish. Most people, however, were satisfied to see the race from the nearest change-over point, and
by far the biggest crowd began to gather, toward sunset, at
the Itonian Gate. They leaned on the ramparts, looking
out across the fields to where the roof of the shrine peeped
among the cypresses, or came down into the roadway for a
closer inspection of the horses.

Alexis, standing at Star's head, stroking the light patch
on her chestnut nose, wished that he had been given almost
any other stage to ride than this one, where he must take
the torch (as it seemed) under the critical eyes of the
whole city. At least Father was not here—but he was somewhere almost as bad. He and Theo, wanting to see Lucian
ride too, had walked out to the next change-over point.
Almost everyone else he knew, even by sight, seemed to
have swarmed like bees around the Itonian Gate.

Hippias was there. That was not surprising. Any kind
of horse race drew him like a charm. He was moving
among the competitors now like a show judge, here lifting a
hoof to examine it, here drawling some question about a
pedigree.

Alexis stiffened as he drew near. Hippias, resplendent
this evening in a silver-gray cloak and scarlet boots, moved
round the mare from the other side, running his smooth

white hand over her flanks as though she belonged to him.

Did horses always know? Lucian was fond of saying they did. Then Star should have laid back her ears and shown her teeth! But she did not. She liked the caress, and swung her head round to nuzzle the man who gave it. So much, thought Alexis, for a horse's judgment of human character.

"Not a bad little mare," began Hippias in a patronizing tone. He broke off as he recognized the boy who held her bridle. Alexis gave him stare for stare. "Quite astonishing, the class of person who rides for his division, these days," Hippias murmured insolently, and passed on. Alexis knew the meaning of that dig. Citizens of the richer grade did their military service in the cavalry, supplying their own horses. They had places of honor in public processions, and thought of themselves as a class apart. If Hippias had his way, only the sons of such men would be picked for the torch ride.

The sun was down now behind the dark ridge of Aegaleus. The crimson and yellow were draining from the sky. A pale green, pricked by one silver star, was slowly taking their place. Soon the trumpet would sound from the starting point. He must think of nothing but the race, forgetting Hippias and his sneers. He must ride all the better, to show Hippias that mere ancestors and wealth did not always produce the best horseman.

"Come on, girl, steady, girl," he murmured soothingly to the mare. Someone gave him a leg up. He settled himself on the square of blanket which served as saddle and nudged Star with his heels to move her out to the edge of the course.

"Stand back, please," the stewards were crying, but nobody as yet took much notice. When the trumpet was heard in the distance and the streaks of fire were seen moving through the dusk, then would be time enough to clear the course. Ten nervous boys sat their horses amid a shifting, chattering crowd.

Suddenly Alexis was aware again of Hippias, not five yards away, with his back turned. His high-pitched, affected voice had sunk to a confidential murmur. Usually he talked as though he did not care if the whole world heard; as though, in fact, he was quite anxious to give it the benefit of his opinion. Now, on the other hand, he spoke so low that Alexis caught only an odd phrase.

"—extremely dangerous!"

For a moment Alexis thought he meant the race. Some of the parents had wondered if it was a good idea for inexperienced boys to go galloping over the countryside in the dusk. But Hippias was no parent. Perhaps he had lent some valuable horse and was now wishing he had not? His companion's reply disposed of that theory.

"It was worth the risk. Anyhow, there's not much risk in this light—and it's getting darker all the time."

So, the darker the safer, eh? Alexis pricked up his ears, but he could catch no more. It had been a strange remark— and there was another strange thing. The man talking to Hippias was wearing the broad-brimmed hat of a peasant pulled well down over his face. What gentleman would wear a hat like that—what gentleman would wear any sort of hat, except in the worst of weather or on a long journey? Yet the man's voice, so far as Alexis caught it, was cultured and Hippias was treating him with much more respect than he would have shown to a peasant.

Were they planning some dirty work in connection with the race?

It seemed a fantastic thought. Hippias might be the type to cheat at games and he *might* be very anxious for his own division to win the race, though it was quite a small affair really, reckoned among the sporting events of the year. But,

with ten teams competing, and eighty horses running altogether, what possible trick could ensure that his team won?
All the same, Alexis determined to watch out for him and
his companion when the moment arrived.

Just then the trumpet pealed faintly across the twilit
fields. A murmur ran through the crowd. "Clear the
course!" cried the stewards, twirling their rods. "There
they go!" called the people on the battlements. "See the
torches!"

Soon even those standing in the roadway could make out
the twinkling points of flame, stringing out across the darkening landscape from left to right. Now one would vanish
for a moment behind a cluster of trees or into a dip in the
ground; now two or three would merge together into one
flaring comet, separating again as individual riders drew
ahead or dropped behind; now the watchers could trace, by
a momentary hesitation, where a torch had passed from
hand to hand at the changing point.

"Stand back!" begged the stewards. "Give the boys a
chance—clear the course!"

The leading riders had turned the first angle and were
galloping straight for the Itonian Gate. The torches shone
bigger and brighter, but they were all dancing together, and
it was impossible to guess the spaces between them. At last
the road was clear of all but the competitors. The crowd
was ranged along the ditch, a pale mass of faces and
bodies.

"Here they come!" yelled a voice from the battlements.

A hush fell, everyone waiting for the warning shout of
the first rider. Now they could hear the rumble of hoofs.
The cry came, a breathless triumphant yell from the boy
leading:

"*Acamantis!*"

Amid a murmur of disappointment and delight, the next
member of the Acamantis team edged forward. All the

other boys grew tense with anxiety. It was nerve-racking to
wonder which name would be shouted next or whether it
would be lost in the growing hubbub.

Here came the first rider, pounding along, his horse a
black shadow, his own head and shoulders lit by the golden
halo of the torch he held aloft in his left hand. For the last
hundred yards he had to ride close under the city wall. It
was lined with bawling faces. For the time being even
the gravest citizen forgot dignity and restraint.

"Here you are!" called his waiting comrade. "Acamantis
here!"

For an instant, as the torch was exchanged, the crowd at
the gate was lit up by its flickering light. It shone on glossy
horseflesh and waving arms, on eyes straining with excitement and dark cavernous mouths stretched in the act of
cheering.

What Alexis caught, in that moment, was a glimpse of
the stranger standing with Hippias. It was a striking, unforgettable face. There was something about the set of the
jaw which no beard could quite cover. And the beaked nose,
the overhigh cheekbones—

The man bent his head, so that the brim of his hat cast
a shadow over his face. Then the torch which had lit up
the scene so briefly went dancing down the Phalerum road.
With a shock Alexis realized that the next two riders were
thundering toward him, and with an even greater shock he
heard one of them shouting the name of his own division.
He urged Star into position.

"Leontis here!" he yelled.

But the next rider, two lengths ahead of his rival, was
the Pandionis boy. He swept out of the dusk on a bay geld-
ing, transferred the torch faultlessly, and plunged aside to
a standstill. By then Alexis had seized his own torch and
Star was streaking down the road. The cheering faded behind.

It was no easy matter, galloping hell for leather through the dark, with the crackling torch in one hand, stretched aloft out of harm's way, and nothing but blanket and bridle on the mare. He was glad of the light from the torch in front. It streamed back, gleaming on the haunches of the gray mare ridden by the Pandionis boy and lighting up the worst ruts and potholes in front of Star's feet. But he must not take the easy way, hanging back and letting the other boy lead. Lucian would have something to say if he did.

"Come on, Star!" he whispered urgently.

The mare answered the pressure of his knees. She sprinted. They drew up to the silvery tail that streamed back in their faces. They edged up, inch by inch, on the left side of the gray. They were level now. Sparks gushed from the torches, other sparks flew from the road below, loose stones spurted to left and right, the tall black trunks of the poplars seemed to reel back as they turned a bend, faces leaped from the gloom and vanished again, voices shouted and were cut off in mid-cry . . .

"Pandionis!"

"Leontis!"

Suddenly he realized that the other boy was shouting too, answering the crowd. There was a mass of people in front—heavens, it must be the change-over point already! Just in time he remembered to call the name of his division. Star made a last effort, drew in front of the gray. For the first time he realized how much they had both caught up on the leading team. They were just passing the torch, thirty yards in front.

"Leontis here!" That was Lucian, almost screaming with impatience.

Alexis reached him a good length ahead of the gray. But they fumbled the exchange somehow, and that slight advantage was lost. Lucian started a length behind.

"Bad luck," said Father, catching Star's bridle and helping Alexis to pull her to a standstill.

"It was my fault," said Alexis. "After all that practice
too! But I was so excited—"

A slave came out of the darkness. Alexis recognized him
as the Thessalian groom from the farm. He slid from Star's
back, patted her neck gratefully, and handed her over. He
must find Lucian and apologize for making such a mess of
the exchange. He started to walk along the road as soon as
the last of the ten riders had gone by.

Soon he heard voices calling the result across the fields.
Pandionis first, Leontis a close second. The gloom was alive
with people walking back to the city. He heard several
voices he knew, and asked about Lucian. At last he met a
boy who answered, with some embarrassment in his voice,
"I think he's gone home the other way."

"Thanks. I see," said Alexis flatly.

He walked a little farther toward Phalerum, though it was
pointless now. He did not want to turn back with the other
boy. He preferred to be alone in the warm, velvety darkness,
with only the grasshoppers singing on either side of the
road. Not, he reflected ruefully, that there was much to
sing about.

6

Alexis decided, first thing next morning, to get hold of Lucian and apologize for his fumbling. It was a pity Lucian took everything so seriously, but it was people like him, after all, who won victories and got things done. He waited in the street and caught his friend on his way to lectures. Lucian was learning higher mathematics (nobody quite knew why) from an old professor who had recently come from Asia Minor.

"Look," Alexis began uncertainly, "I'm sorry about last night."

"That's all right." Lucian's tone was cool.

"I got flustered and——"

"Oh, forget it. These things take a lot of practice. I shall do much more myself if I'm picked next year. There's a lot in what my father says—'if a job's worth doing at all, it's worth doing well.' "

"Yes." Being anxious to make things up, Alexis bit back the remark whch sprang to his lips: if Lucian's father was

so fond of proverbs, had he never heard of the most popular Greek saying of all, "*Nothing in excess*"?

"I mean," said Lucian, "everyone's entitled to go his
own way. One either takes sport seriously or one doesn't. If
a fellow prefers fooling around with girls——"

"If you imagine that's what I've been doing——"

"I don't think myself as clever as you, but I'm not a
complete fool."

"I can assure you——"

"I'd rather you didn't. I don't expect you to tell me your
personal affairs—not now—but there's no need to tell me
lies, either. You see, I'm just not interested." With that
Lucian hastened away in pursuit of the higher mathematics.
Alexis stood on the street corner, flushed with fury.

When one feels unjustly treated, it is natural to look
round for sympathy. For years past, the two of them had
always confided in each other. When things went wrong,
they had grumbled together in corners. "It's a shame . . .
'Tisn't fair! . . . He played a dirty trick on you. . . ."
How many conversations had run along those lines! Alexis
felt lost now, wondering where to turn. Then suddenly he
knew.

Corinna . . . she had seemed a decent sort, someone he
could talk to. And it would serve Lucian right for sneering.
If he was so certain Alexis had been seeing her, why not
give him some real grounds for his belief?

There was, of course, the little matter of Milon's morning lecture on the art of the orator. Alexis snorted. If he
couldn't convince his own best friend of the simple truth,
how would he ever persuade a political meeting or a
jury? Other boys cut lectures sometimes. This morning
he'd do the same.

When it came to finding Corinna, he felt shy. He walked
past the inn several times, hoping she might see him from
an upstairs window. The inn looked clean and bright with

its pink-washed walls and blue paint—he wondered if there were really bugs in all the beds, as there were supposed to be in every inn? Then for a long time he lurked round the public fountain, hoping she might come for water. But the group of girls and women, filling their jugs from the lion-head spout, made him blush with their jokes and gigglings. After being asked for the third time for whom was he waiting, he decided it would be less embarrassing to take his courage in both hands and ask for Corinna at the inn.

This called for courage. Respectable people seldom went to inns—if far from home, they stayed with friends. If Father heard that he had even set foot inside, there would be trouble on a grand scale. His mind was so full of this thought that he never considered whether his call might also embarrass Corinna.

With a nervous glance to left and right, he slipped through the archway into the courtyard. A glorious smell of cooking met him. Such smells, he thought, the gods must sniff on Olympus, when a heavenly banquet was being prepared.

An immense woman emerged from the kitchen doorway, ladle in hand. She towered—but even more, she bulged. Her face was scarlet from squatting over the hearth, but it was a kindly face and her small eyes twinkled. "Well, sonny?" she demanded in a voice which would have quelled a ship's mutiny.

"I'm looking for Corinna," he faltered.

"So am I, most days. The child's here, there, and everywhere, like one of them lizards. Still, as it happens, this morning I know she's gone to Cephalus."

"The sculptor?"

"That's him. Masons Street. Here," she said, diving back into the kitchen and emerging with a small cake, "try one of these, sonny."

"Thank you very much."

It was still warm from the hearth. It was sweet with honey, and stuffed with chopped nuts and raisins. He munched it gratefully. "Excuse me," he said, "are you Corinna's mother?"

"That's right. Gorgo's the name. How did you guess?" She wheezed with laughter. "Family likeness?"

"Oh, no," said Alexis, more hurriedly than was quite flattering. It was hard to connect the slim girl with this good-humored mountain. "It was the cake—she said what a wonderful cook you were."

Gorgo nodded her gray head, well pleased. "Best cook in Syracuse, they used to say. And I can tell you, cooking in Syracuse *is* cooking. They don't know how to eat here. Have another?"

"No, thank you ever so much. I must be going."

"Please yourself." Gorgo paused in her kitchen doorway. "There's a good old saying, so I suppose I'd better stick to it—'them as asks no questions is told no lies.' " And with another wheezy laugh she vanished.

Alexis wondered if that was a proverb Lucian's father ever quoted. If he did, Alexis felt sure, it would not be with such a delicious rascally chuckle, or such a twinkle in his eye.

He crossed the market, that fascinating place, where (with sufficient money) you could buy anything from fish to flutes—or even flute players. Not that anyone would want a full-time flute player. If you needed one for a party, you hired her for the evening, along with the dancing girls. Alexis had no special interest in any one department, he liked the whole bustling place. He liked to see the fishmongers slapping down their glittering fish, and the sudden rush of customers when the bell rang to announce that the fresh catch was in. He enjoyed the noisy arguments

between the breadwomen, cursing each other one minute
and bellowing with laughter the next. He loved the bright-
ness of the vegetable stand—the great golden pumpkins
and the wrinkled green cucumbers and the feathery carrot-
tops, the purple grapes and the mounds of polished apples,
and the flowers in season, lilies and roses, violets and jon-
quils and hyacinths. He loved the market because he loved
life, in all its humor and beauty.

But this morning, having no mind to meet Father or anyone who might report his absence from lectures, he slid
through the market as quickly as he could, using the
shady colonnades which ran round the sides. Five minutes
later he was knocking on the sculptor's door. "Is there
a girl still here?" he asked the salve who opened it. "Her
name's Corinna, Gorgo's daughter, from the inn——"

"Is it the young model you mean, sir? Straight ahead,
sir, and across the yard. She's with the master in his studio."

Too late to turn back. He had meant to inquire, then wait
about till she had finished her errand. But the slave had already bowed him into the passageway and closed the street
door. Evidently Cephalus did not mind visitors when he
was working. Anyhow, famous as he is, he can't eat me,
Alexis told himself. So, squaring his shoulders and remembering that he was the son of Leon, champion athlete and
war veteran, he went in.

The studio was an untidy little workshop, the floor lit-
tered with stone chippings and trodden lumps of clay.
Cephalus worked both with chisel and mold, as could be
seen from the unfinished pieces ranged along the walls, some
in stone and others in bronze. Just now he was modeling.
He was a bald little man with a dusty gray beard, muscular
arms bare to the shoulder, and surprising hands that
seemed almost to have an independent life and brain of
their own as they ran deftly over the clay, pinching and
stroking it into shape. Every few moments he paused and

looked, with eyes half-closed and head on one side, at the girl standing on the pedestal.

Corinna was wearing a short, girdled tunic of Spartan style. Her bare legs were bent in the action of running, one hand grasped a bow, and her head was turned and held high, as though her eyes were scanning the distance.

"Artemis!" burst out Alexis without thinking.

Corinna twitched at the sound of his voice but did not turn to look. She stood there as if frozen.

Cephalus turned. "All right, my dear," he said in a chirpy little voice. "Rest. No one could hold that pose for long." He laid his head on one side and studied Alexis with narrowed eyes. "Show me your side face. H'm. Yes. I don't remember asking you to come and see me. But you might do very well."

"Do?" Alexis echoed, mystified.

"As a model for Pan, if I ever want one. Isn't that why you came?"

"Oh, no, sir!" Laughing, Alexis explained his call. "Though I'd be very honored, sir, and I'm sure my father would, if you ever wanted to do a statue of me."

"It wouldn't be a statue of *you*," Cephalus corrected him, "any more than this is going to be one of Corinna. It is, as you said, Artemis the Virgin Huntress. Corinna is posing because she is, in most respects, the type I want. I realized that as soon as I saw her in the street. But you're not perfect, my dear," he said, wagging his finger at her as she sat smiling on the pedestal, "and a goddess *must* be perfect. Your chin's wrong—but never mind, I know another girl who'll give me the chin I want. And your ears are quite, quite impossible for Artemis. I shall have to get the ears from Lysilla, or maybe Gyllis."

Corinna laughed her silent laugh, pretending to be hurt. "If my features are so bad, why don't you get one of them to pose for the whole statue?"

"Ah, if you'd only seen them, my dear! Imagine one of them ranging over the mountaintops with a pack of hounds! No, you're the model I want, with all your faults."

"Thank you, sir!" she said with mock humility.

"Well, that's enough for this morning. You're tired, and I must be off to the market place. Yes, my boy," he said, turning back to Alexis, who had begun to study some of the work along the walls, "that statue you're looking at—it's one of the best portrait statues I've ever done. It was commissioned to stand in the middle of the city, but it's stayed here in my studio ever since it was finished, years ago."

"Whose is it, sir?" There was a tense note in the boy's voice. He was staring at the head of the statue and they could not see his own expression.

"Magnes. The politician. You may remember, he was exiled. They say he plotted with the Spartans. He wanted to overthrow the democracy and set up a dictatorship."

"No! Not in Athens!"

"So after that, naturally there was no more talk of honoring him with a public statue. It'd be silly, when he daren't show his own face here under pain of death."

"I don't like him," said Corinna frankly, studying the sculptured features. "Why do you keep it here?"

"Oh, you never know, my dear. Magnes has some powerful friends among the rich families. In politics anything may happen. You're down one day and up the next. We may yet live to see Magnes back in Athens, dictating to the lot of us—and where would I be if he found I'd thrown his statue on the rubbish heap?"

Alexis was silent as he walked out of the studio. He was thinking hard. The statue had the unforgettable set of jaw, the hooked nose, and the too-high cheekbones he had seen last night below the peasant's hatbrim. The whole face was that of the man who had been whispering with Hippias.

7

I thought you wanted to talk to me," Corinna complained, with an amused twitch at the corner of her mouth, "but we've walked the length of the street and you haven't said a word. For real lively conversation, give me a statue."

"Sorry. I've just had kind of a shock." Alexis hesitated a moment, then took the plunge. "It's like this. That man Magnes who wanted to set up a dictatorship——"

"Oh, the man with the awful face!"

"Yes. I could have sworn I saw him last night, out by the Itonian Gate, during the torch ride."

"Suppose you did."

"But don't you see—didn't you hear what Cephalus said? He was exiled years ago."

"Was he?" She had obviously not listened very carefully to the conversation in the studio. But now, suddenly, the meaning of what he was saying penetrated. She turned eagerly. "Oh! Then what is he doing in Athens?"

"That's what I'd like to know," he said grimly. "I wish I knew what to do."

"Tell your father."

"H'm . . . It would take some explaining, how I came to be in Cephalus' studio."

"Your father wouldn't approve of me."

"Well . . ."

"Don't apologize! Athenian boys aren't supposed to be friends with girls. That's why I nearly fell off my pedestal when you walked in just now. I *was* pleased to hear your voice—I haven't really talked to anybody since that day in the den. By the way, how's your handsome friend?"

"Not very pleased with me," said Alexis, forcing a laugh. "His beautiful nose has been put out of joint—or so he feels."

"What by?"

"You."

"*Me?*"

"Yes, You see, we've been friends for ages. Only—you know how it is—you don't want to be with anybody *all* the time, however much you like them. You want to get right off on your own now and then. . . . You do know the feeling, don't you?"

She nodded her dark head. "You've seen where I go."

"Well, Lucian doesn't seem like that. He doesn't like reading, and he's always so awfully active—wants to be doing things every minute, and expects other people to do them too."

"Still don't see where I come in."

"Just this, if I want an hour to myself, he jumps to the conclusion that I'm really with you, that I'd *sooner* be with you than him——"

"How silly!" she commented demurely.

"Absolutely crazy," Alexis agreed with more warmth than tact. "I swore to him I hadn't seen you since that first day, but he was so angry he wouldn't believe me. So I thought, darn it, I'd give him something to be angry about——"

"And here you are?"

"And here I am."

She stopped short and turned to face him. The blood had rushed to her cheeks, and her gray eyes were flashing.

"Thanks for telling me! I know Athenian girls are treated like dirt, but you're not going to do that to me. Using me just to make him angry—like picking up a toy to tease a child——"

"Oh, heavens!" he cried despairingly. "I didn't mean that at all. Everybody misunderstands everything."

"Then we'll have no misunderstandings between you and me, anyway. If we're to be friends it'll be because we want to be friends, not because we want to annoy somebody else."

"Of course——"

"And no snippy talk, just because I'm a girl and a foreigner and Mom keeps an inn?"

"No," Alexis promised sincerely. "But you ought to promise something too."

"What?"

"No sneers against Athens. If the city's good enough for you to live in, it's not fair to keep running it down."

Corinna nodded slowly. The anger had faded from her cheeks and she looked at him with more respect. "All right. A boy ought to stick up for his city. I wouldn't think much of you if you didn't. I won't sneer, but——" she gave one of her quiet laughs—"I can make intelligent criticisms? After all, free speech is the thing in Athens!"

"You're learning," he said with a delighted grin. "Live here a year or two, and you'll be one of us." But as he said it he knew it could never be true. Though born in Athens, she was an alien and would never be anything else. It was the hardest thing in the world for an alien to get Athenian citizenship, and for a woman it was unthinkable. She could not even marry an Athenian; the law forbade it.

They walked on. People stared. At the next corner, where the street grew busier and they could hear the hum of the market, Corinna said, "Better separate now. I know you feel awkward walking with me——"

"No, really——"

"Let's be honest—or nothing. It's the way things are here. I don't want to get you into an argument with your father. And I don't want to break up your friendship with Lucian. Say you'll make it up with him and no more silly standing on your dignity?"

"All right, but I shall be friends with you too."

"Then come up to the cave tomorrow, can you? I'll give you a flute lesson!"

"That's a bargain." They parted at the corner and he watched her out of sight. Some people might call her an alien—a little more than a guttersnipe—but she stepped through the crowd as proudly as the virgin goddess Artemis.

The strange incident of Magnes gave Alexis an excuse to tackle Lucian at the gymnasium that afternoon. It was Luican's turn to bring flowers and decorate the statue of Hermes, patron god of gymnastics, which stood in the cloister.

"Can I help you?" Alexis offered.

Lucian glanced round. "Oh—" He looked surprised. "If you like. I'm trying to fix these hyacinths *here*, and then evergreens round the whole lot."

"I see. Lucian, I want to tell you something."

"What?" Lucian was on his guard.

"Nothing about us. Something really important. I've got to tell somebody, but there's no one else I can trust."

"Go ahead," Lucian invited him, obviously pleased.

Alexis told him about the stranger, and how a chance visit to Cephalus' studio had revealed his identity. It meant bringing in Corinna, of course—he was not going to lie to Lucian—but he told the full truth, how he had not seen the girl previously but had gone looking for her that morning because he was annoyed with Lucian. His friend listened gravely. "I'm sorry," he said. "It was rotten of me not believing you the first time."

"Let's forget it. This is much more important—and I'd never have found out about Magnes if we hadn't had the fight."

One of the boxing coaches came quietly down the cloister on bare feet. "Don't be all day with those flowers, young Lucian! And you, Alexis, why aren't you spear throwing?"

"Coming, sir!" they cried in unison. Before they parted, Lucian to the ring and Alexis to the field, Lucian said, "Wait for me after, and we'll think what to do."

"Fine." Alexis darted out into the sunshine, feeling happier and freer than he had for days.

"Of course, there may be nothing in it," said Lucian as they walked slowly home. "I suppose you couldn't possibly have been mistaken?"

"No. It was such a striking sort of face. . . . And it isn't as though I heard about Magnes first and then imagined I saw him at the torch ride. It was the other way round. And what I heard them say was rather suspicious, though I didn't understand at the time."

"It would make sense," Lucian agreed with a thoughtful frown. "Hippias said it was 'extremely dangerous'—meaning it was dangerous for Magnes to be in Athens——"

"That's what I guess."

"And Magnes said it was worth the risk, and there wasn't all that risk, because it was getting darker all the time."

"And people wouldn't recognize him! Remember, he had a peasant hat, but he didn't talk like a peasant. And he was hobnobbing with my dear friend Hippias!"

"I don't like it," said Lucian. "I heard about Magnes when I was a kid. You don't get exiled for nothing."

"It must be awful. Having to leave everyone you know, everything you care about. . . . I just can't imagine what I should feel like if I was exiled."

"I can't imagine your doing anything to *get* yourself exiled. People who plot against the city deserve all they get. They certainly don't deserve to go on living here. Well," said Lucian in a brisker tone, "let's decide what to do."

"Yes, we'd better."

"You can't tell your father, because that means too many explanations—how you came to be in Cephalus' studio when you should have been at Milon's class——"

"I think we ought to keep Cephalus out of it altogether if we can," Alexis broke in shrewdly. "Mightn't it make trouble for him with some people—narrow-minded people, I mean—if they heard he was keeping that statue?"

"That's his lookout. He shouldn't keep the statue of a traitor."

"But it *is* a work of art, Lucian. One of the best he's ever done."

"Can't help that. He ought to scrap it."

"Well . . . we needn't quarrel over that." Alexis forced a laugh. "Could you tell *your* father? I mean, tell him I think I caught sight of Magnes—you needn't say how I knew his face. I might easily have known him by sight before he was exiled. Then if your father could drop a hint to some official, they might check the story—and they'd be able to keep their eyes open if Magnes shows himself across the frontier again."

"I've a better idea. My uncle's on the Council—the one who lent us the horses. I'll tell *him*. Best to work through the proper channels," said Lucian solemnly.

"Yes, of course."

And they walked on, feeling that the matter was settled so far as they were concerned, and that they had acted with a thoroughly grown-up sense of responsibility. Then, as they crossed the market, they noticed Hippias, and once again, almost without realizing it, Alexis let himself be sucked back into the dangerous currents which seemed to eddy round that gentleman.

"He needs watching," Lucian muttered darkly. "If Magnes is up to something, Hippias is in it too."

"Say—suppose we do the watching?"

"How do you mean, exactly?"

"Keep an eye on him, and who his particular friends are. And if we find out anything fishy, tell your uncle."

"Not a bad idea! *You'll* have to be careful, though—he knows your face."

"M'm . . . yes. Still, no harm in seeing who he's with now—he won't notice me in the crowd."

Hippias was standing in the middle of a group. There were several other smart young men, two or three much older ones, and a fringe of lads in the background, among whom Lucian and Alexis were able to slip unnoticed. They were not surprised to find that a discussion on politics was raging. But it was not quite the kind they were used to overhearing, about particular leaders or topical questions before the Assembly. It was a discussion of general theory.

Hippias was holding forth with his usual self-confidence. "The whole idea of democracy is feeble," he was saying. "It's based on the wrong principle, to begin with."

"How, my dear young friend?" They could not see who

had spoken, for there was a pillar in the way. But his voice
was that of a much older man—gentle, persuasive, utterly
unlike the high-pitched, affected tones of Hippias.

"Oh, it's quite easy to explain," said Hippias airily.

"So much the better. I'm not very clever." A ripple of
amusement ran round the group. Hippias hurried on, unwilling to lose control of his audience.

"Well, we often compare governing the country with
navigating a galley—we talk about 'the ship of state'——"

"An excellent comparison."

"But we'd look like fine fools if we went to sea on 'democratic principles'!" Hippias sneered as he pronounced the
phrase. "If we kept having debates on when to hoist sail
and cast anchor, and voting who was to steer—we'd soon
be shipwrecked that way." This time the laughter was on
his side.

"Who then *should* take the helm, my dear Hippias?
Judging from what you said earlier, I imagine you'd give it
to the man with most wealth stowed away in the hold?"

"We-ell. . . ." Hippias wavered, suspecting a trap. "He
would have the strongest motive for taking care of the
ship."

"Would he also have the greatest skill as a steersman?"
inquired the gentle voice from the other side of the pillar.
"Have you ever been in a storm at sea, Hippias?"

"Of course! Many times!"

"And I presume you've always insisted that the helm
should be taken out of the hands of the poor sailor and
given over to the wealthiest passenger? You'd feel much
safer that way?"

There was such a roar of delight from the listeners that
the retort of Hippias was lost. Alexis saw him, flushed and
stammering, quite thrown off his balance by the unexpected
twist of his argument.

"Who is it?" Alexis whispered to Lucian. "I must see."

They edged round the pillar till they could see the man whose quiet, almost humble questions were giving Hippias so much trouble. "Oh," said Lucian, with some disapproval, "it's that man Socrates."

Alexis had seen him before—he was too well known a character for anyone to miss. He stalked the streets like a pelican, barefoot even in the winter snow, a grotesque figure with a snub nose and a tublike stomach bulging the folds of his robe. But Alexis had never been able to observe him closely, to see the good-tempered twinkle in the rather prominent eyes and the humorous lines cut deep in the weather-beaten face. And never before had he listened to the voice which, it was said, could cast a spell over those who heard it.

Hippias lost his temper. He could not bear it when the laughter turned against him. "I should have known better than to argue with you, Socrates," he said sarcastically. "We all know you're the wisest man in Athens—in fact, the wisest in the world."

"Oh, no," the older man rebuked him gently with a smile. "I'm not wise at all. Though perhaps in one respect I'm wiser than—" He checked himself for a moment and concluded tactfully, "than some people I meet."

"Indeed? Then there is some limit to your amazing modesty?"

"I am wise only in this respect, my dear young friend: I know nothing, but I *know* that I know nothing; some people know nothing, but they believe that they know a very great deal."

It was done so delicately, so courteously, that Hippias was given every chance to withdraw from the battle in good order. But he could not recover his lost temper so easily, and the appreciative chuckles of the other young men did not help him. He snorted, muttered some hasty, ill-mannered excuse, and flounced away. Socrates smiled apologetically at those who remained.

"Now you know why I'm sometimes nicknamed the Gadfly," he said with a chuckle. "It seems to be my natural mission to irritate and sting—even the noblest and best-bred of animals! And then see how they go plunging away across the paddock!"

Alexis suddenly felt Lucian's hand upon his arm. "Come on," his friend murmured. "No point in staying now."

"N-no, I suppose not. . . ." But Alexis turned away reluctantly. He had heard the voice of Socrates the spellbinder, and he would gladly have stayed listening till suppertime.

8

Freedom . . . new things . . . Alexis had been right to expect great changes in his life when ordinary school days were over. But, he reflected as he lay wakeful on his bed listening to Theo's calm childish breathing in the darkness, he had not realized how deeply those changes would affect him.

He had grown up in a strict but happy home, with plenty of toys when he was small enough for hoops and tops and toy rabbits, with nursery rhymes and bedtime tales, and with treats and outings on holidays. But there had also been discipline, enforced first by his mother's slipper, and then, when he was seven and too old to be looked after by women, by the schoolmaster's stick; above all, and from the earliest years, by the stern voice of Father.

He had been brought up always to do and think the right thing. To carry himself well, to have good manners, and to respect his elders. To pray to the gods and to visit the temples with small offerings at suitable times. And to remember at all times that he was an Athenian, born in a city lying under the special protection of the goddess Athena

and destined, by her favor, to lead all Greece in power
and glory.

These things were not to be questioned or doubted.
They were as obvious as two and two makes four: one did
not even have to go through the form of proving them, as
one did (having been shown how by the master) with a
statement in geometry.

Some things, of course, he had often questioned in his
heart, because he was a natural rebel. Why shouldn't a man
run in the street if he was in a hurry—was dignity everything in grown-up life? And why should Mother have supper in her own room when Father had people in for the evening, instead of the whole family sitting down together as
usual? Why assume that women were too ignorant to take
part in an intelligent conversation?

These questions had remained unasked until lately.
School did not encourage them. At school you learned
yards of Homer and Pindar and the other poets, and you
learned from them all about the gods and ancient heroes,
and what kind of character and behavior to imitate. If
sometimes the poets seemed to contradict each other—and
even contradict themselves—you were not supposed to point
it out. You swallowed the lot, along with the mathematics
and music. It was all true (or you would not be taught it)
and all equally good for you.

The system suited most people. It suited Lucian. It produced fine men like Father. But Alexis was less sure now
that it had quite suited him.

Corinna had given him his first big shock.

She had walked in from the outside world, and every
word she spoke, every glance from her calm gray eyes, re-
minded him that the outside world was a big place, full of
its own wonders and different in many of its ways.

And now there was Socrates, and the young men who
mostly made up his set. . . .

For several days after that first encounter, Alexis had taken every opportunity to hear that gentle, humorous voice again. It was not difficult, because Socrates seemed to spend most of his time talking with friends in public places, and anyone, young or old, was welcome to join in. What talk it was, too! Alexis had never heard anything so fascinating.

Socrates questioned everything. It wasn't that he contradicted people. He just asked patient, humble questions, so that they had to explain more fully what they were trying to say. Over and over again it happened that, when they had finished, they found they had been saying something quite different from what they had intended. Alexis liked it best of all when some pompous individual came along and started laying down the law on a subject he fancied he knew all about. Then Socrates would start off with his meek little interruptions—every one of them like a keen knife, slicing up the man's eloquent rigmarole until it lay before the audience like a fileted fish. Alexis had always been interested in words and their meanings, but never, before he heard Socrates, had he realized how exciting the quest for exact truth could be.

Truth? A fat lot old Milon cared about truth when he taught them oratory! That was another thing Alexis loved about Socrates—his honesty. He was not really trying to score off these people, he was genuinely seeking the truth. But the truth was the last thing that mattered in public speaking, if Milon was to be believed.

"Oratory," he told the class, "is the art of persuasion. People are most ready to believe what they *want* to believe. Therefore, in planning any speech, you will first consider the audience, ask yourself what kind of things these particular men wish to believe, and pick out arguments of that sort. Then arrange them so that whatever you are trying to put over to them will seem the logical result."

Alexis had asked, seemingly innocent, hiding his disgust,

"Please, sir, what about when you have to persuade them of something they don't want to believe? It must happen. Suppose the state's in danger, or taxes have to go up?"

√"A good point!" Milon had his answer. "Normally you work on their desires, but sometimes you must work on their fears. Give them a good fright!" the class laughed. "Paint the danger in dreadful colors—but point out that it would never have arisen if *your* advice had been taken. Distract your audience from the unpleasant truth by attacking the opposition speakers. Show that it was they who landed the country in its predicament, and that your proposal— whatever it is—is now the easiest way out."

"I see, sir." This time he could not conceal his feelings entirely. A little of the irony he had caught from Socrates crept into his voice. "So that's how to become a good statesman, and serve the country?"

"It's how to become a first-class orator," said Milon tartly, "and that's what I'm paid to teach. A swordmaker's job is to make good swords, not worry about the battles they'll be used in."

But he was wrong, thought Alexis, tossing on his bed and waiting for cockcrow; he must have been wrong, only I didn't know how to answer him. Socrates could have done it, though.

Lucian was still keeping an eye on Hippias, but he had nothing suspicious to report. There was no secret about his politics. Like many rich men of aristocratic blood, Hippias belonged to a select club which stood for "government by the best people." There was nothing illegal about that, so long as it did not involve conspiracy at home or plotting with foreign powers—the kind of activity for which Magnes had been banished.

"Uncle made a few discreet inquiries on the Council,"

he told Alexis. "They think it couldn't have been Magnes you saw. He was last heard of in Sparta. Personally, I don't see that that would have stopped him from slipping across the frontier and into Athens, specially at Festival time——"

"I *know* it was the same man."

"Well, they're keeping a lookout for him in the future. I don't think we need worry any more," said Lucian comfortably. "They know what they're doing."

"I hope so." There was some doubt in his voice. Of late Alexis had lost confidence in the eminent personages who guided the fortunes of his country. It was hard to say whether Socrates or Milon had done the more to undermine his faith.

If only Father realized what rotten ideas lay at the basis of Milon's teaching, he would take his son away. Father's pet hero Pericles had been a great orator, but he hadn't followed Milon's methods. He had faced unpopularity without fear and he had told people the unpleasant truth when they needed to hear it. If Father could sit at the back of the lecture room and hear some of Milon's petty little hints, he would have sixty-nine fits. But if he merely heard them from Alexis, and then stormed along to Milon for an explanation, Milon would get around him easily and complain that he had been misrepresented. Milon knew all the professional tricks for deceiving a jury: it would be child's play for him to win over one indignant parent.

But he must get away from Milon. There was something in the atmosphere of that lecture room which stifled him. Socrates had said a fine thing yesterday: "A lie isn't only a bad thing in itself, but it plants badness in your soul." Alexis felt that if he went on for a whole year, listening to Milon's hypocrisy, he would not be able to help growing a little like that himself. "Don't swim in dirty water" was a good rule; if you did, you could hardly expect to stay clean.

If he could not make his father see that Milon was bad, could he at least persuade him that some other professor would be better? But what other? Pondering the problem, Alexis knew that there was only one person he wanted to study under, and that was Socrates. Would Socrates take him as a student? That was the difficulty. Socrates wasn't like the others, he wasn't like anyone else in the world.

There was no harm in asking, though. He felt he could never be afraid of asking Socrates anything. He seized a moment when the old man was, for once, alone—stalking down the road to the public baths.

"Please, Socrates, just a minute——"

"Well?" The great bare forehead bent toward him, the kindly eyes studied him. "What can I do for Alexis, the son of Leon?"

So he remembers my name, thought Alexis, that's something! Socrates had noticed him hanging on the fringe of the group a day or two before, and had asked him. "Please, Socrates," he said breathlessly, "suppose I could persuade Father, would you teach me? And—er—how much do you charge?"

The old man laughed. "My dear boy, do you imagine I take fees from all those young friends you see me with?"

"You . . . you mean . . . you teach them for nothing?" His face fell. Father would not think much of a man who taught for nothing. In this world, he was accustomed to say, you get nothing for nothing. That was why everybody knew Milon was a first-class teacher: his fees were high.

"I teach nobody anything," said Socrates, smiling at his crestfallen look, "so how could I take their money? I have never accepted a fee in my life."

"But you *do* teach us," Alexis protested. "I've learned ever so many things, just listening."

"Indeed?" Socrates hesitated. If Alexis had been a year or two older, and less modest in his manner, he might have found himself undergoing an examination which would have left him like a pricked bladder. But Socrates liked boys, and spared him. "I'm glad to hear that," he went on with only the faintest irony, "but you mustn't give *me* the credit. Everything is here from the start—" He tapped the boy's brown head with a blunt forefinger. "All I do is help a little to bring people's ideas to their lips, so they're put into words and can be tested properly."

"I—I'm sorry, Socrates. I really thought——"

"Nothing to be sorry about, my dear boy. If you like listening to our little discussions you will always be welcome."

"Oh, thank you! You don't think I'm too young or anything?"

Socrates smiled. "The pursuit of wisdom is a long, long chase. If you feel ready to start, the sooner you are off, the better." And he went on his way to the public baths.

"Tell me some more about him," Corinna demanded. They were sitting in the cave mouth a few days later. The lilac was over, but the quarry was spangled with oleander blossoms. She had just given Alexis a flute lesson and now, before going on to read the play he had brought—it was one by Sophocles today—they were refreshing themselves with fruit and talk.

"Well, he *looks* a little comic," Alexis admitted, "rather like a satyr——"

"Ought you to say a thing like that up here?" she interrupted, half jokingly, half nervously. She was not so superstitious as Lucian, nor yet as scientific as Alexis was becoming under the influence of his new companions. It might be awkward if there *were* satyrs and if one of them popped up now with his half-human, half-goatish body and long horse's tail, vexed at being compared with a philosopher.

"Nothing to worry about," Alexis assured her. "They're only something imagined by the poets, Socrates says."

"Go on about him, then."

"He's a most surprising person. He's got a great fat stomach, yet he's amazingly fit. I think he was quite an athlete when he was young, and he still keeps in training. He did very well in the army, too, and he was recommended for a medal, but he made them give it to someone else—incidentally, he'd already saved the other man's life during the battle."

"Did he tell you all this?"

"Heavens, no! I heard it from the others."

"What are they like, the other boys?"

"You'd hardly call them boys—I'm by far the youngest —they're young men really. There's Xenophon. He's a real sport. I don't think he's terribly intellectual, though—he thinks more about horses and dogs and the army—but he's good fun to talk to. And there's Plato. He's twenty. He's a wonderful all-round person, because he's good at sport, especially wrestling, yet he writes poems and wants to write a tragedy. Like me," Alexis added dolefully, "though a lot of use it is for me even to think of it if it means competing against people like him."

"I don't know that I would like Plato," she answered sympathetically. "He sounds just a bit *too* perfect."

"Oh, you would, though!" Alexis assured her, anxious to be fair. "You'd approve of Plato's view."

"How?"

"He thinks women are equal to men and ought to have the same education."

"Good for him!" Corinna clapped her hands. "Tell me more."

And he went on telling her about Socrates and his wonderful young friends until the lengthening shadows warned

them it was time to start back for the city, carrying with
them the book which had never even been unrolled.

When he got home his mother greeted him with a worried look, and Theo said, "Father's been looking for you."
Nico caught his wrist and murmured, "What have you
been up to, Alex? They never tell me anything."

"I don't know, honestly, Nico—"

Just then Father came striding out into the courtyard.
Now for it! Alexis braced himself for the attack. Had some-
body seen him slipping into the tavern to speak to Corinna?
Or—

"Alexis!"

Father's voice was firm but quiet. He was making a
real effort nowadays to remember that Alexis was not a
small boy. He no longer ordered him about. He tried hard to
discuss things man to man, but the old habit of authority
was hard to shake off. Even Philip, when home on leave,
was apt to feel the rough edge of Father's tongue.

"Yes, Father?" said Alexis, going to meet him. They
stood under the fig tree. Parmeno came through a doorway
and bobbed back again. The yard became strangely quiet,
but Alexis felt sure that Theo and his sister were lurking
somewhere, straining their ears to catch the low-voiced
conversation.

"I'm very sorry to hear," Father began, "that any son
of mine should form a thoroughly undesirable association."

So he had heard about Corinna. But what a way to
speak of a perfectly harmless friendship! The blood
rushed to his cheeks. He tried to answer Father in the same
controlled voice. "Why is it so thoroughly undesirable?" he
asked.

"Surely you realize?" said Father patiently. "This man
Socrates . . . his name's a byword throughout the city."

So it wasn't Corinna after all, but Socrates! "What's wrong with him, Father?" he stammered confusedly.

"He's an atheist, for one thing—doesn't believe in the gods. He's the ruin of any young man he lays his paws on."

"That's not fair——"

"It's true, Alexis. I don't blame you altogether for not realizing. He's a sly old man, and he has a great fascination for young people. He seems to take away all the decent ideas and standards they've been taught before, and to fill their heads with the most poisonous rubbish instead."

"B-but—but—" Alexis floundered, trying vainly to find some connection between the Socrates he knew and the man Father was describing.

"Alcibiades was one of them, and what happened to him? Ruined a brilliant career and sold his country to the enemy! He wasn't the only one to turn out badly, either. And what sort of youth has the man collected round him now? Plato—whose uncle Charmides is one of the most dangerous antidemocrats in Athens! Xenophon—who openly admires the Spartan system! Do you think I want a son of mine mixed up with that crowd?" Alexis opened his mouth, but Father raised his finger to command silence while he finished. "You're very young, luckily. You can drop out at once, and no harm done. But understand, the association must stop. Now. Socrates and his ideas are the ruin of any young boy who comes into contact with them." He dropped his hand affectionately on Alexis' shoulder. "It's not going to happen to you, though—I care far too much to let you run the risk."

9

Rhoo-rhoo, *rhu-rhu-rhu-rhoo!*

The mellow call of the wood pigeon echoed against the walls of the marble quarry. Crouched in the undergrowth Alexis saw something bright flash into view above. Corinna was there in the cave before him, as usual. She was wearing crocus yellow. She stood in the cleft, peering this way and that.

Ha-ha-ha!

The cry of the jay burst mockingly from the lilac tree at her feet. She smiled and bent forward. "You can't take me in with that noise, Alex! Though I will say you fooled me for a minute with your wood pigeon. Come on up."

Grinning, Alexis set his foot in the fork of the tree, took her outstretched hand, and sprang lightly up onto the ledge beside her. "You're a plague," she grumbled. "If you'd been a real wood pigeon you'd have made another for my collection. I haven't seen or heard one round here."

She was counting all the different birds who came to the

quarry. Woodpecker, cuckoo, magpie, jay, kestrel, francolin
. . . the list was growing. They had once seen a kingfisher,
where the waterfall came trickling down; and they suspected there was a nightingale. They had even wondered
whether they dared stay out all night sometime and hear
its song, but they had decided it would not be worth the
trouble—in more senses than one.

"Mom would give *me* nightingales!" Corinna had said
regretfully. Gorgo was an easygoing parent, broad in
mind as well as broad in beam, but she drew the line at all-
night escapades. So, thought Alexis, would Father, who did
not even know of Corinna's existence.

"What have you brought to read today?" she demanded.

"We're going to have a writing lesson." He pulled a roll
of clean papyrus from his tunic and laid it down, together
with a supply of reed pens and a knife to split them, and
a tiny bottle of ink which winked jet black when the
stopper was taken out.

"Oh, good! What am I to copy?"

"I'll dictate something . . . something I know by heart."

"Euripides? Homer?"

"You'll see."

"I like to take some interest in what I'm writing!"

"I hope you will."

"Schoolmaster!" She put out her tongue. Corinna's manners were not improved by living in a tavern atmosphere.

He split one of the reeds, sharpened it, and passed it to
her. She lay down on the smooth rock floor, reclining on
her left elbow, knees drawn up, and prepared to write. He
stood in the cave mouth, arms folded, looking away toward the city and the distant sea. Slowly and clearly he began to dictate:

"Heavy the news, Achilles, lord, I bring . . ."

He stopped after about twelve lines. It was slow work,

but Corinna's writing, like her speech, was certainly improving. She formed the graceful letters as lovingly as she would have embroidered a dress. He stooped and pointed out her few mistakes. "What do you think of it?" he asked casually.

"Think of it? Oh, the speech, you mean? It's nice. But it's rather gloomy, isn't it?"

"Well, darn it, it's meant to be a tragedy! You wouldn't expect the messenger to be laughing his head off. He's come to tell Achilles that his best friend is dead."

"Yes. . . . Of course, I like comedies much better. Like that one you brought by Aristophanes—where the women all go on strike till their husbands promise to stop the war."

"You mean *Lysistrata*."

"That was it." Corinna recorked the ink bottle and studied her handiwork once more. It was hard to tell whether she was admiring the verse or her own writing. He licked his lips nervously. His heart jumped when she looked up and said, "This *is* lovely, all the same. What play does it come from?"

"*Patroclus*," he grunted.

"Never heard of it. Who by?"

"Alexis, son of Leon."

"Alexis—" Light dawned. She scrambled to her feet. "You mean *you*? Oh, Alex, how clever! I never realized——"

She was so genuinely impressed, he could not hide his own satisfaction. "Glad you like it." He smiled.

"You *are* awful! Suppose I hadn't, and I'd said so, I might have hurt your feelings, and——"

"That's why I didn't tell you. I wanted an honest opinion."

"Can you remember any more?"

"All there is. I think I've done two or three hundred

lines. Had to carry it in my head—no chance to write at home without everyone asking questions."

"Then you must write it down here! Make it up in your head, bit by bit, and copy it out when you come. The cave's quite dry, so we can keep it here, and the ink and everything."

"Yes, that's—" He was about to say, that's what I thought, but changed his mind. "That's a fine idea," he said warmly.

"But first you must say all you've made up so far," she commanded. "I shall enjoy it lots more, not having to write it down." She sat down again, her back against the rock, her hands clasping her knees. She never stirred until his voice dropped into an everyday tone and he said, "That's all I've done."

"Oh, Alex," she murmured, "you *must* have been miserable when you were thinking of all that!"

He laughed awkwardly. "Just like a girl! Straight to the personal aspect. What about it as poetry? It's not me speaking, remember, it's Achilles, and Thetis, and——"

"It's you. Every word."

He saw it was no use arguing with her. "I have been rather in the dumps lately," he admitted.

"About Socrates? Not being allowed to go and hear him?"

"Yes. And other things. I thought it was going to be such fun, growing up. But it seems pretty rough. I wish I was older still, doing my military service. Perhaps I shall hate that too." He laughed, more naturally this time.

"There's one thing," she said slowly, "you can always laugh at yourself, Alex."

"Just as well. I know I'm a joke. But unlike most jokes, the older I get, the funnier I find myself. Ah, well—" he stooped to roll up the papyrus— "it may not be immortal verse, but it made me feel better, getting it off my chest."

"It's good. I loved it, though I didn't understand all of it. But I wish you'd write a comedy."

"You can't write to order," he explained. "You've got to be so full of an idea that it just bubbles out."

They stayed an hour or two at the cave, playing the flute and talking. They started back in good time, so that they could follow the winding banks of the Ilissus instead of the dusty road.

"I love the country," said Corinna. It was full summer now. The small cornfields were ripening to gold, studded with scarlet poppies. There were marigolds like polished brass, and borage blue as the sky. In the long grass hundreds of grasshoppers kept up their incessant hum. Alexis teased her, recalling what someone had once said: *Happy are the grasshoppers—their females have no voice.*

"Yes," she said blandly, "and listen to the racket they make! Nearly as bad as a lot of men."

They walked on. The stream was shallow now. They took off their shoes and paddled through the cool water. The plane trees made a blue-green tunnel of shadow overhead.

"Yes, I love the country," he agreed, coming back to her former remark. "If I were Father, I should live on the farm and only go into the city for festivals."

"Wouldn't his business go to pot?"

"That would hardly matter—he being a potter!"

She laughed. "Of course—you had told me."

They went a little farther. Then he stood still, the water frothing round his ankles. "Some people in front—listen, you'll hear them talking." She cocked her head. Above the steady murmur of the stream there was the less regular murmur of men's voices. "Golly!" Alexis whispered in sudden excitement. "It sounds like Socrates, but it can't possibly be——"

"Why shouldn't it be?"

"But he never sets foot outside the gates, he's not interested in Nature, he says——"

"All right," said Corinna, after taking a few steps forward and peering through the branches, "if you say it's impossible, of course it must be! But there's a snub-nosed old gentleman lying there on the grass, and if it isn't Socrates—"

Alexis was full of alarm. He had been dreading the day when he must meet the old man again, but to run into him out here would be much more embarrassing than any encounter in the busy street. "We'll have to creep round," he muttered.

"Creep up, you mean," she retorted.

"What?"

"I want a close look at this wonderful person—I want to listen. I'm not going to miss a chance like this."

"But Father said—" For once he found himself talking like Lucian.

"Your father didn't want you to get mixed up with the crowd and get a bad name," she argued. "He's not going to worry if you happen to overhear half a dozen words. Or are you so weak-minded that half a dozen words can ruin your character?"

Alexis gave in, not unwillingly. Whatever Father said, he admired Socrates: there must be a misunderstanding somewhere. It could not be really disobeying Father just to sneak up and listen for a little while, without showing himself.

"Who are the others?" Corinna whispered as they peered between the leaves.

"That's Plato next to him. The other good-looking one is Xenophon. I think the other man's named Phaedrus."

"M'm . . ." said Corinna with feminine appreciation. Plato and Xenophon were as handsome as their master was ugly. Plato was the younger: while powerful and athletic in body, he had the fine sensitive features of a poet. There was something soldierly about Xenophon: he looked a man of action.

What weighty subject the men were discussing the two friends were never to know. Something crashed suddenly through the bushes. Corinna let out a scream. By the time she had realized that it was only a young hound and that, far from trying to bite her, he was the friendliest creature imaginable, Xenophon was on his feet and parting the branches. It was too late to escape. Feeling rather foolish, they stepped out onto the sunlit grass, the hound weaving delighted circles round them.

"Why, Alexis!" said the old man, sitting up. He glanced at Corinna. "I was wondering why you had deserted us. Need I inquire further?" His deep-set eyes twinkled. He had not always been a calm philosopher. Long years ago he had been wild and passionate, and he had not forgotten.

"It wasn't me that's kept him away," said Corinna in her blunt Doric.

"No? Perhaps I may guess then? Your father, Alexis?"

Alexis gulped. "Yes . . . Father doesn't understand, I'm afraid. . . . He—he thinks you're a bad influence on me——"

"You see, Socrates?" broke in Xenophon in a meaning tone, as though some such subject had been discussed before. He sat down again on the grass, fondling his hound.

"And how am I a bad influence, my dear boy?"

"Well, he says you don't believe in the gods."

"He says that?" Socrates wagged his head thoughtfully.

"They say it all over Athens," Xenophon interrupted again. "Some day it will land you into serious trouble."

"Sit down," said Socrates, "if only for a little while, so that I may explain." Corinna obeyed readily, Alexis after a brief hesitation. But, he reflected, he could hardly be so rude as to refuse. "Have you never heard me quote my favorite line of Homer?" demanded Socrates. "*In due proportion to thy means pay honor to the gods.*" He chuckled. "Does that sound like atheism? Xenophon and I were at an all-night party until sunrise—he will tell you that I prayed to Apollo before I went off to breakfast and my bath. And altogether, so far as prayers and offerings are concerned, you can assure your father that I do my duty just as Homer says I should."

"But you criticize Homer at other times," said Xenophon. "That's what's so dangerous. We have no sacred books as the barbarians have, but Homer comes pretty near."

"Of course I criticize Homer, and all poets, down to Euripides!" Socrates turned back to Alexis. "You have been brought up on these poems, and you get your ideas of the gods from them?"

"Well, naturally——"

"And how are the gods shown as behaving in these poems? Don't they quarrel like children, overeat and overdrink, steal, flirt with other people's wives, and, generally speaking, carry on as no decent mortal man would think of doing? Isn't Zeus shown as taking his heavenly scepter by force from his own father? What sort of example is that, hey? What would *your* father think of it?"

Alexis grinned. "I guess that's one of his favorite stories."

"If there are gods, then, surely they're better than mortals, not worse? Surely nobler than anything we can imagine? So the poets, however entertaining, are shocking liars. Try to make your father understand, if you discuss this again, that disbelieving old stories is not the same as disbelieving in the gods."

"I wish you could make all Athens see that!" said Xenophon forcibly.

"I do my best. I talk to everyone I meet. But there are a lot of people in Athens, and life is short!"

"Exactly. And you may find it shorter still, if you go on making enemies at this rate."

"I? Make enemies?"

"Do you think people like being made to look foolish, Socrates? One day it's that fellow Hippias, another day it's one of the democrats—you don't care who it is."

"Of course I don't. I'm concerned with ideas, not personalities. And surely if people find they have been holding wrong ideas, they should be very grateful for any help in finding out their mistakes?"

"Human nature doesn't seem to work like that," said Corinna shrewdly.

Xenophon shot her a grateful glance and said in a serious tone, "Some of us are really worried for you, Socrates. If people properly grasped your ideas it would be all right. But for every man who does, there are hundreds who depend on gossip and rumors. Then you're made fun of in plays, and the whole audience gets a thoroughly wrong impression of your views." He turned to Plato. "You're so clever with your pen, why don't you write a comedy and put Socrates into it? But the real Socrates, as he is."

Plato shook his head and smiled. "Not my line, I'm afraid. I write lyrics. Some day, perhaps, a tragedy. But not comedy."

"There is no essential difference between tragedy and comedy," Socrates began slyly, in an effort to start a general discussion and draw the conversation away from himself. But Xenophon was not having that.

"You should make an effort," he told Plato bluntly. "I wish I could."

"I'm sorry. But a man should do what his nature fits him for. I couldn't possibly compete with Aristophanes.

Now a dialogue sketch possibly, something in the style of Sophron but introducing the philosophic ideas of Socrates—"

"Unfortunately the theater doesn't put on philosophic dialogue sketches in the style of Sophron! It isn't books we want—they take time to circulate, and they never reach the mob. We want a play that every man in the city would see next year, something that would explain Socrates and make him popular."

"What a deplorable idea!" said the old man, his heavy body shaking with laughter.

"It might save you from serious trouble, though—exile, or worse. But as it seems to be out of the question, *please* try to be more tactful, and don't make any more enemies."

"I can't change my ways, Xenophon. The gods seem to have sent me as a gadfly to stir up Athens, and there it is."

Alexis and Corinna felt, though reluctantly, that they must be going. They said good-by and, as it was late, struck across the fields toward the road. Corinna was eager to give her opinion of Socrates and his friends, but she found Alexis quiet and thoughtful. "What are you thinking about?" she asked.

"*The Gadfly*," he said slowly. "What a title for a comedy!"

10

Summer was passing. Sickles flashed in the fields, the dry gold corn went rustling down. Along hillside terraces the grapes darkened and lolled in heavy bunches. White dust hung behind the oxcarts. The trees stood still and waited, their leaves crisp and withered, for the gales of autumn.

Meanwhile Alexis worked at his comedy.

It was strange how that chance meeting with Socrates and Xenophon had set him off. As though a spark had been struck and set to a fire laid ready. He had wanted so much to write a tragedy—he had refused to face the fact that a great tragedy could be written only by one who had lived and suffered, not by a boy fresh from school. Now he knew that his *Patroclus* had been sentimental, unoriginal, no more than a fluent imitation of playwrights he admired. He had written it because he wanted to write *something*, not because he had anything special to say.

With *The Gadfly* it was different. He had something definite and urgent to say: "This is Socrates as he really is. It isn't Socrates who's a danger to Athens—it's the conceited people, the superstitious, the wordy windbags and the hypocrites, the men he's all the time exposing for what they are."

It could not be said like that, of course. It had to be set out in absurd situations with exaggerated characters, with puns and jingles and jokes, skits and parodies and topical references. Always the touch had to be feather light—"it's just the same in cooking," Corinna assured him, "you ruin some things if you're heavy-handed." He found her a great help. He recited each passage to her before he wrote it down. "Trying it out on the dog," she called it good-humoredly, but she was far more critical than any dog would have been. "Hold on," she would say, "you're getting a bit *serious* here." He would argue at first, and then see that she was right. His feelings had begun to carry him away, and the scene, like a cake in the oven, had gone heavy and "sad." Luckily a play, unlike a cake, could be changed bit by bit during the baking. The heavy parts could be cut out and replaced, and extra fruit stuck in as required.

"But honestly, Alex, I don't know how you do it," she told him. If she was sharp in her criticisms, she was as warm in her admiration. He needed her encouragement. Nobody else knew about the play. Lucian was much taken up with his own affairs just then, training for a big sports festival and posing as a model for a sculptor; somehow, though they had made up their quarrel, their friendship had never quite gone back to its old heart-to-heart basis. Father would not budge in his disapproval of Socrates and insisted that the year's course with Milon must be finished. Those stolen hours with Corinna, sometimes in their den at the quarry, sometimes in Gorgo's hospitable kitchen, were the happiest he knew that summer—those and the

hours when he was alone, thinking out fresh line.
play and lost in the fantasy world of *The Gadfly*.

"I don't know how you think of such things," Corin.
said, "and put them all together."

He tried to explain. It was not easy. School had given
him a thorough grounding in poetry and drama, and he
had always done well at writing exercises in the styles of
famous authors, seizing on their particular tricks and man-
nerisms or twisting their best-known quotations to a
slightly different form and a very different meaning.
"Parody always goes down well in the theater," he assured
her with the full weight of a boyhood's experience. "Better
than at school," he added with a chuckle. "The master used
to say I was too disrespectful to the great poets—I got
beaten for that, once."

There had been plenty of acting and recitation at school,
and he had always enjoyed that. Then, until his voice had
broken, he had sung in the boys' choral festivals, and he
still joined in the less solemn celebrations at Harvest
Home, when the boys went in gangs from house to house,
singing comic songs and collecting presents. All this practice, added to years of theater going and a study of published plays, had given him the technical knowledge he
needed for a comedy; but it did not explain why that
comedy should be any better, when finished, than a clever
boy's effort, "good for his age" yet still hopelessly amateur-
ish.

As the weeks passed into months, however, and the first
roll of papyrus became covered with shining black script—
"thirty feet of fun," Corinna called it—even the young author himself began to wonder if *The Gadfly* might not be
something more.

Corinna valued those hours as much as he did. As he
came to know her better he realized that she had her trou-

bles too, though she grumbled less about them. Somehow that first meeting by the river, when Lucian had mistaken her for a nymph, had left him with a lingering impression that she *was* like a nymph in some ways; that, while she was certainly solid, mortal, laughter-loving, sweet-chewing flesh and blood, she was also free as any spirit of the woods and streams to rove about and do as she liked. She was, of course, by comparison with Nico and the sisters of the boys he knew. But she had her own worries.

"I *hate* living in an inn," she blurted out one day.

"Why? I'd have thought it was kind of fun—plenty of life, fresh faces, people coming and going." He was thinking of the place as he saw it himself. Gorgo's kitchen was a wonderful center for the gossip of the city. Little did she know how much it had contributed to *The Gadfly*—how many of her own robust jokes and racy comments had been noted by the boy who sat quietly in the corner waiting for her daughter. It was from Gorgo, with her endless stories of guests and servants, her passion for scandal, and her earthy sense of humor, that he had drawn his best material for the broader parts of his comedy. If it was ever to stand a chance of production, he knew it must contain something for all tastes. It was all very well being witty and subtle (there was a deliciously satirical scene in which a long-haired dandy, suspiciously like Hippias, was shown up as the real danger to the country) and he could pour into the choruses all the lyric beauty he could ever have put into a tragedy, but there must also be jokes obvious enough for the simplest spectator.

"It *was* fun when I was a child," said Corinna, wriggling her toes in and out of her sandals. "But I feel different now. Some of the guests are horrible. They're so . . . well, familiar. Mom says it's only their way and they don't mean any harm—says I'm too high and mighty and we

can't afford it in our trade. We have awful fights sometimes."

This was news to him. He had heard Gorgo scolding a
slave or a dishonest guest, but she had always seemed kind
to Corinna and most welcoming to himself.

"Naturally, she'd be nice to you," said Corinna.

"Why 'naturally'?"

The girl looked embarrassed. "Oh, well, she does *like*
you, Alex, she likes you a lot, but I'm afraid it would be all
the same if she didn't."

"I don't understand."

"You're good class, you see. And your family are citizens. You'll be a citizen yourself in a few years."

"What on earth does that matter?"

"Mom says always keep in with citizens. Wherever we've
been, it's been the same. 'They're the people who can kick
us out,' she says, 'we've always got to remember that—
we're aliens, we're dirt to them.'"

He was shocked. "But I don't feel like that about you—
or your mother."

"No. But you must try to understand how Mom looks at
these things. She's had a terribly hard life, she's always
been poor, she's always had to struggle. And she always
will. You see, Alex, for our sort there isn't really much future."

He did not answer for a full minute. It was difficult to
know what to say. He had never thought about the problem before. Now, comparing Corinna with Nico, he saw
what she meant.

It was quite easy to see, in his mind's eye, what his sister's future would be. In a year or two she would be engaged to some man of decent family. Father would arrange
it, but he would never make her have anyone she did not
like. The day before the wedding she would solemnly dedi-

cate all her old toys and girlish possessions to Artemis; on the next evening would come the triumphant procession to the bridegroom's house, with everybody singing and pelting them with grain; and in the morning crowds of visitors and heaps of presents. After that Nico would have a home and slaves of her own. The years would pass, she would have babies, and eventually—comic as the very thought now seemed—she would be a grandmother, honored and loved and obeyed.

There would be no such future for Corinna. She *might* get married—Gorgo might fix up something with an alien living in Athens. But he wouldn't be anybody much—or he'd have to be completely blinded by Corinna's good looks if he was willing to take his bride from an inn.

"It is difficult," he said awkwardly. "Especially not having a father."

"Mom's at me to go out with the flute girls," she muttered.

He sat up, full of consternation. He knew that one of Gorgo's side lines was to book flute girls and dancers for private dinner parties. Plenty of respectable people engaged these entertainers and it was quite a recognized thing, but the girls themselves, whether free or slaves, were not highly thought of.

"You'd hate that!" he said.

"Don't worry," she retorted fiercely, "I'd sooner starve than go out making an exhibition of myself like that."

"I'm surprised your mother suggested it."

"She says it's time I did something to earn my keep, and it's that or slave's work around the house. There's not much a girl *can* do. And of course," she added moodily, raising the instrument to her lips, "I can *play* this thing."

Listening to the plaintive air he nodded admiringly. She certainly could.

Sometimes the play got stuck. He lost heart. He felt it was no good. Why trouble to finish it? Fifteen hundred lines! What a labor, all for nothing! The minister who chose plays for production would not look twice at it. Then something happened which showed him that he must move heaven and earth, not only to get the play finished but to get it accepted for the Spring Festival.

"You must miss your class with Milon tomorrow morning," said Father at supper.

"Oh, yes, Father? Why?" he said readily.

"I'm taking you to the law court. It's good for a boy to go now and then and see how things are run. Lucian's coming with us. His father may be on the jury, so I said I'd look after him."

"Good! That'll be interesting. What's the case, Father?"

"Alleged blasphemy."

"What's alleged blasphemy?" demanded Theo. He spoke the last word with gusto, enjoying the explosive sound.

"Blasphemy means speaking or acting disrespectfully to the gods. Alleged means they *say* the man did it, but they must prove it before he can be punished."

Alexis had gone pale, and when he spoke he found it hard to keep his voice casual. "Who is it, Father?" He was relieved when Father named someone he had never heard of.

"Should be an interesting case," said Father. "Very seldom it comes up. Must be years since there was one quite like this. Maybe it's a pity," he added darkly, "that it doesn't come up a little oftener."

They started for the market place straight after breakfast, and found a big crowd assembling—most of the five thousand men whose names were on the jurors' register for the year.

"They're divided into ten lists, five hundred each," Father explained. "Nobody knows till the morning of the trial which five hundred will serve on the jury—the officials are drawing lots now to decide."

"What a waste of time, making everybody turn up!"

"There's a reason. By leaving it to the last moment, they make it impossible to get at the jury and bribe them."

Alexis thought for a moment, then asked in a quiet tone which had a faint echo of Socrates: "Wouldn't it be better to find a jury of honest men who could be relied on not to take bribes?"

"Much better," Father agreed, "but much harder!"

At that moment there was a hush while the herald gave out which jury was to serve, and then a general movement as the others went about their business and the chosen jurymen lined up to get their colored sticks of office and their tickets entitling them to a day's pay at the end of the trial.

"It *is* the panel that my father's on," said Lucian, rather pleased. "Come on, sir, they always try their cases in the Middle Court. Let's get good places up against the rail."

It was another half-hour before all the preliminaries were over, the sacrifices offered to the gods, the jury settled on their mat-covered benches, the general public herded behind the rail by the police, and the president enthroned on his platform between two lower platforms from which the prosecutor and the defendant would speak.

"That box the clerk is opening contains the charge and the evidence," Father whispered. "The papers in the case have been sealed up ever since the first private hearing. They call the box the 'hedgehog.'"

"Why?"

"No idea," Father admitted. "Just an old name."

"I'll ask my father tonight," said Lucian. "I should think *he'd* know."

The case began. Alexis was glad to find that, though Father might not know why the sealed box was nicknamed the hedgehog, he was well up in all the other details of the law. His whispered explanations made everything clear and he was able to answer all the questions the boys put to him.

Alexis found himself even more interested in the subject of the case than in the procedure for trying it. The accused was a schoolmaster, charged with teaching his boys that the sun was not really a god, Apollo, driving a flaming chariot across the sky, but an enormous mass of white-hot matter, almost as large as Greece. Nor was the moon a goddess, Apollo's sister Artemis, but another lifeless mineral body, shining by reflection of the sun.

"He must be crazy," Lucian hissed. "Can you imagine such nonsense?"

"Crazy to teach it in a school, maybe," Alexis agreed. "Maybe not so crazy to believe it himself!" He took care not to let Father catch the last remark. Lucian's shocked expression was quite enough.

When the schoolmaster stood up to make his defense, he denied teaching his class that these theories were true. He had mentioned them, certainly. He believed that boys should be trained to think for themselves and to distinguish between the right and the wrong. After all, he was not the first to bring forward the theories—anyone was free to buy the books of Anaxagoras the philosopher, in which they were fully discussed.

There was a hostile murmur from the jury. Under the circumstances, the mention of Anaxagoras was tactless. "*He* was exiled for these theories when I was a young man," Father explained. "It caused a stir, because he was a friend of Pericles, but even Pericles couldn't save him."

The case ended. The jury filed past the voting urns. Each man had two tokens, one for "guilty" and the other for "not guilty." He dropped the one he wished to use into the first urn. The waste tokens clinked into the other.

The result was "guilty," by a large majority. The prosecutor then demanded a sentence of exile. The schoolmaster, supported by his wife and three children, all in their oldest clothes and weeping to win sympathy, begged the jury to let him off with a heavy fine.

"Why doesn't he suggest a smaller one?" asked Lucian.

"Well, the jury must choose one penalty or the other— they can't fix it themselves."

"I see. If he said too little, then, they'd be sure to vote for exile?"

"Exactly."

Alexis was relieved when the result of the second vote was announced. The schoolmaster was to be fined. "But of course," said Lucian, "his school will be ruined—no one'll send their children to a scoundrel like that."

Outside the court they met Lucian's father. He said he had voted with the more merciful majority. "You see," he told his indignant son, "this schoolmaster fellow is only small fry, really. The case was no more than a tryout, just to test public opinion."

"Do you mean, sir," said Alexis with sinking heart, "that they'll be bringing more cases? Against—against other people?"

"Well, it's high time we did, my boy. You youngsters have got to be protected. And there's far too much dangerous nonsense talked nowadays. Free speech is all very well, but. . . ." He shrugged his shoulders. "One has to go carefully in these matters. It's so different from an ordinary criminal case. Depends more on public opinion, and that's apt to shift from month to month. When we go after the really dangerous fellows, we need to be quite sure of a conviction. They're tricky customers, and if they got acquitted it would do far more harm than if they'd been let alone in the first place."

"Let's hope this case will be a warning," said Father. "I don't *like* interfering with any man's liberty to speak his mind—"

"There'll be some more cases all right in due time," Lucian's father assured them. "Some people are just waiting to have a crack at these clever fellows." He was almost smacking his lips at the thought. Alexis saw in his mind's eye a sickening vision of Socrates standing up to face five hundred "gentlemen of the jury" as self-satisfied and prejudiced and deaf to new ideas as Lucian's father. Socrates would never cringe and beg for mercy. If he ever came to be sentenced it would be exile at least, more likely death.

11

Upon my word, Alexis, I don't know what we're to do with you!"

It was clear that Father was angry. He had flung himself down on his couch beside the supper table, but he made no movement toward the dishes at his elbow. Mother and Nico and Theo, sensing the atmosphere of storm, sat very quiet and straight on their chairs. Alexis, who was learning to take his meals in a reclining position, like a grown-up man, raised himself on one hand and eyed Father with considerable anxiety.

"I can't think what you *do* with your time! You don't spend it on the sports field, I do know."

"I've been walking a lot, Father, and swimming and—"

"The boy's all right," said Mother. "The whole family can't be champion athletes."

"I don't expect them to be." Grudgingly, Father accepted the food offered him. A delicious smell of roast pork filled the lamplit room. It was not often they had meat, but today was a festival and they had had to sacrifice a small pig. That meant burning the thigh bones and some fat on the altar and giving the priest a choice cut, but everything else went back to the kitchen. What a pity, Mother was thinking, that Leon had met that man in the street tonight of all nights, when they had such an extra-special supper and only wanted to enjoy it in harmony!

"I long ago gave up any hopes of Alexis in that direction," said Father, "but I did expect he would be a credit to the family in his own way. I seem to have been mistaken."

"What have I done wrong now, then?"

"What have you done wrong now? Don't take that defiant tone with me, boy!"

"I'm sorry, Father, I didn't mean——"

"In my young days we didn't cross-examine our elders, we kept quiet till we were spoken to. I suppose you pick up that kind of habit from people like Socrates. Have you been running round that man again, after what I told you months ago?"

"No, Father," he answered indignantly. He had often been tempted, seeing Socrates and his group in the market place or at the gymnasium, but he had kept away from them obediently.

"Socrates?" said Theo with interest. "Isn't that the old man who's so blasphemous?"

"Yes," said Father, and "No!" said Alexis in the same instant, so that on any other occasion they would both have burst out laughing. As it was, they almost glared at each other across the supper table.

"Ah," said Theo wisely, "then he's only—er—*alleged*."

"This has nothing to do with you, Theopompus," Father reproved him, but not too severely. Theo was in high favor. He had won a race a few days ago. Father turned back to his less satisfactory son. "Just as I was coming home, I met Milon."

"Yes, Father?"

"He says your attendance is irregular, your work only half prepared, and that your whole attitude in the lecture room varies from the indifferent to the insolent!"

"I'm sure Alex wouldn't be insolent," said Mother. "He doesn't *like* Milon, of course."

"One can't help being bored sometimes," put in Nico, flushing. "Surely it's Milon's business to make his classes more interesting?"

"Thank you very much," said Father, a dangerous glint in his eye, "but I should prefer Alexis to speak for himself. I send him to Milon—one of the best-known teachers in Athens—so that he can learn to do just that."

"Best-known, perhaps, but not best!" said Alexis. "Milon is an old humbug. What's worse, he multiplies quickly—like other kinds of bugs. Every year he turns out young humbugs like himself, till soon the whole city will be crawling with them. Do you realize that man Hippias is one of his ex-pupils? I don't want to be like that. But I've never been insolent to Milon, whatever he told us to do. Only critical."

"Critical! It isn't your place to criticize, at your age. All you have to do is to work hard, use the brains you have, and learn what you're taught."

"But, Father, I shall *never* make an orator——"

"How hard have you tried? At least you could attend all your classes regularly, spend proper time on your exercises instead of mooning round the countryside by yourself, and treat Milon with proper respect. Or have I got to face the fact that I overestimated your ability in the first place—that one of my sons is going to turn out a failure, a nobody like my old uncle? There seems to be bad luck about the name Alexis."

"Your Uncle Alexis is a good man," said Mother firmly.

"If he is poor, it is because he has always been too kind to other people, too unselfish."

"You mean Uncle Paintbrush?" asked Theo. "Oh, I love him."

"Unfortunately," retorted Father, "his reputation does not stand so high in the city as it seems to in this house. I hope all my sons will make more of their lives than he has."

There was a rebellious silence round the supper table. Everyone loved Father's old uncle. He was always known to the children as Uncle Paintbrush, because he spent most of his life at the pottery, painting the new-made bowls and vases with black varnish and etching little scenes upon them. The nickname suited him. Great-uncle Alexis would have sounded far too formal.

"Well," said Father, "if Alexis fancies he is going to get away from Milon's classes by slack behavior of this kind, he is very much mistaken. He will not only finish the course. I have persuaded Milon—he was really most helpful about it—to take him on for a second year when the time comes."

Autumn was darkening into winter. Against the leaden sky the cranes flew south to Egypt. After them came the rain, scudding before the wind. The crags streamed and shone, the leaves fluttered down, the Ilissus boiled through the ravine.

"I suppose we shall have to give up the cave soon," said Corinna regretfully. "It'll be so cold. And the afternoons are drawing in so, there's not much time to get home before dark."

"We could light a fire, then it'd be quite cozy inside."

They were huddled in the narrow entrance, watching the rain as it hissed down through the creaking branches.

"It'll soon be spring again," she consoled him, "and the Drama Festival. You must cheer up and get your play finished."

"It *is* finished."

"What? You've done that last scene?"

"And rewritten the chorus I wasn't satisfied with. I lay awake half last night, hammering away at it in my mind."

"No wonder you look as if you'd been whitewashed."

"I'm all right."

"Is the chorus?"

"I thought it was. I'm not so sure now."

"Let me hear it, then."

He pulled out the roll of manuscript and read the verses into which he had poured all his pride and love of Athens. His voice was shaking when he came to the end:

> "Violet the crown of our city,
>   And sea-green the hem of her robe!"

There was a silence so long that he was afraid Corinna had not liked it. Then she said, very quietly:

"It's beautiful now. It must be a wonderful feeling to be Athenian . . . to know you really *belong*. If that chorus doesn't bring the audience to their feet——"

"No audience will ever hear it," he interrupted bitterly. He rolled up the manuscript. "It'll never get accepted."

"But it must, Alex! It's good—the whole play, I mean. You're not going to tell me there'll be so many better ones sent in, you won't even get a place?"

"I mean that the minister won't look at a play written by a boy straight from school! I was a fool not to face the truth before."

She looked at him hard. Then she took him firmly by the shoulders and shook him until his wet hair flopped in and out of his eyes. "You've been talking to Lucian!" she said accusingly.

"His father, actually."

"You've told him about *our* play?"

"Of course not! I made a sort of roundabout inquiry. He's awfully well up in rules and regulations. He said a very young writer wouldn't stand a chance. 'You see, my boy—' " With a wry smile Alexis launched into a parody on Lucian's father: " 'A minister is spending public money on these productions, and he must always remember he is answerable to the—er—electorate. However promising he might consider the manuscript in his—er—private judgment, in his public capacity he would be extremely hesitant, he would view with the utmost caution——' "

"Flapdoodle," said Corinna tersely.

"But I'm afraid he's right."

"Are you sure? There must be some way around."

"Of course, I could put the manuscript away for a few years and send it in when I'm twenty-one. Some of the jokes are so old, anyhow, they'd keep that much longer!"

"Do be serious, Alex! You sound as though you didn't care at all."

"That's how a comedy writer *should* sound, isn't it? The light touch."

The rain had stopped. The clouds had parted and suddenly the whole landscape glistened with the pale gold of autumn sunshine. The far-off sea came back into the view, its gray brightening to green. The mauve bulk of the Acropolis hill rode high above the rooftops. "Look," she said, and quoted softly:

> "*Violet the crown of our city,*
> *And sea-green the hem of her robe!*"

She smiled, a calm certainty in her eyes. "That play's going to be acted," she said. But, as she admitted later, she had not the faintest idea just then how it was to be done.

Within two days she thought she had the answer. She could hardly wait to ask Alexis what he thought. She tried to catch him on his way to Milon's. She dared not risk his father's wrath by going to the house.

She missed Alexis, but saw Lucian. Her impatience conquered her caution. She darted after him and twitched his tunic. "Lucian!" she panted. He turned, his bright dark eyes hostile. "What on earth do you want?"

"I've got to see Alex. Will you tell him?"

Lucian looked down at her. She could read the mental processes at work behind those regular features. She was a bad influence . . . a girl, and low class at that . . . something one's best friend should be protected from.

She did Lucian an injustice. For he answered, after a moment's consideration, "All right, I'll tell him."

"Thanks ever so much!"

"I—I'll have to be getting on now. I'm late." And with a nervous glance down the street and a dark flush mounting to his temples, Lucian departed at a most athletic pace. She went back to the inn, determined not to go far away until Alexis came.

"You can make yourself useful," her mother quickly informed her. "Don't hang about there in the yard. What d'you want wearing your best saffron yellow? It'll be dirty in no time. You run up and change, my girl, and come right back and do something for your living!"

"Oh, all *right*, Mom." She went rebelliously, not because she minded helping in the kitchen—it was a cozy place, these sharp wintry days—but she did not want Alexis to call and find her smudge-nosed, red-faced, and in her tattered working dress. But Gorgo was not to be argued with.

It seemed an endless morning, but gradually the shadows shortened in the yard. People came and went. At every footstep she wiped her face and peered out cautiously. It was never Alexis.

It was close on dinnertime when she had the last of the false alarms. This time it was a rather grand slave. He demanded Gorgo, and, with a lordly wave of his hand, indicated his master in the background. Gorgo peeped, took in the aristocratic features and expensive cloak and boots with an experienced eye, and bustled out into the yard, wiping her hands on her dress. "You want to see me, sir?"

"Ye-es. Your name *is* Gorgo, I suppose?"

"That's right, sir."

"H'm. We-ell, I've penetrated to your somewhat unsavory lair because I'm giving a rather particular supper party, and I'm told you're one of the best caterers in Athens. Do Syracusan stuff and all that?"

Gorgo beamed. "Very kind of you, sir, I'm sure. I was six years in Syracuse, and though I say it myself——"

"Quite." He checked her with an elegant gesture. His rings flashed in the sunshine. "Do your best, my good woman, and it won't be the last order you get. Do you do the entertainment side as well—bit of music, dancing, that sort of thing?"

"Leave it to me, sir! I can get you some of the best in the business—nice girls, too, and clever. There's Chloe, she juggles wonderful, as well as dancing, and Praxilla does the real acrobatic stuff, don't know how she does it, *I* couldn't, but of course she's got more the figure for it than what I have—" Gorgo heaved with laughter and her eyes almost vanished into her crinkled face.

"Quite. I leave the details to you. Don't send a team of old hags, but remember, looks aren't everything. I had a flute girl at one party, pretty as a picture, but she didn't know one note from another." His eye fell on Corinna in the doorway. He pointed to her with his stick. "She one of your girls?"

"My own daughter, sir. *She* plays the flute lovely—" Gorgo stopped, seeing Corinna's furious scowl. "But she's too modest about it," she went on. "Of course, she's young. I don't want her to start going out to parties just yet." Gorgo had told many lies in her time, but never one so reluctantly.

"Pity," said the young man. He gave her the date and the number of guests.

"And what might the name be, sir?"

At that moment Alexis came hurrying through the archway. He saw Corinna and smiled.

"Hippias," said the young gentleman. He had his back to the archway. Neither he nor Alexis was aware of each other.

Hippias! Of course—the affected dandy whom Alexis had made fun of at the theater! The man Socrates had taken down so neatly, the man Alex suspected of being mixed up with the exiled plotter Magnes. . . . She acted promptly. She signaled. Alex looked blank, then took in the situation and popped back into the archway like a rabbit into its hole.

Hippias swaggered out, slave at heel. Gorgo turned reproachfully. "You missed a real chance there! Some mothers would have *made* their girls go. Those are the folks to get in with. Far more use to you than that boy! Don't suppose *his* father gives a bang-up party like this, not in ten years——"

"Oh, keep quiet, Mom!" she begged in agony. Alexis was coming back, grinning all over his face. Gorgo stared at him and, without a word, flounced back into her kitchen.

"Dodged him nicely," said Alexis. "Lucian said you wanted me?"

"Yes." She ran to meet him, forgetting possible smuts on her nose. "I've been asking around a bit," she whispered urgently. "Do you know how old Aristophanes was when his first play was done? No older than you! He sent it in under someone else's name—he was friends with an actor, and this man——"

"But I'm not friends with any actors!"

"What does that matter? Any grownup would do."

He thought for a moment. "I wonder who'd do it for me? It's not everybody who'd put his name to a boy's play."

"Wouldn't Xenophon? He wanted this sort of play to be written."

"He *might*—for the sake of Socrates. But he has ideas about being an author himself. . . . I don't know about him."

"Well, surely somebody would help? Your father would get some friend of his?"

Alexis bit his lip. "No," he said firmly. "Father's the last person I'm going to about this. He'd be wild with me for wasting my time."

"Well, of course, if you don't really *want* to get your play sent in——"

"I do. I'm just thinking. I've got it. Uncle Paintbrush!"

He went to see his great-uncle straight after dinner. Everyone else in the pottery was having a restful hour for digestion. The old vase painter, as he had expected, was squatting in a corner, hard at work.

"Uncle, please, I want your help!"

"What have you been up to?" Mild blue eyes were lifted questioningly. Then the elder Alexis stooped to his task again. He was decorating a large wine bowl. He had painted it all over with glossy black varnish. Now, on the inside, he began drawing fine lines to expose the red clay beneath. Stroke by stroke he drew a nymph with fluttering draperies, then a jovial satyr in most determined pursuit. It was amazing, the boy thought, the sureness of touch with

which he drew in one figure after another on the difficult
concave surface inside the bowl. Each was perfect. Each
eye and finger and bare toe, etched in red against the shiny
black. How clever Uncle Paintbrush was! How could people say he had "done nothing with his life" when he had
been making such pictures for fifty years, and his work
must have traveled to every city round the Mediterranean?

"Well?" the old man prompted him encouragingly, starting a second and particularly wicked-looking satyr who had
a subtle resemblance to the younger Alexis in his wilder
moods.

The boy explained. "You see," he concluded, "if only
you'd agree, it would be so appropriate."

"Appropriate?" Uncle Paintbrush touched in the satyr's
hoofs, then his shaggy thighs and a beautifully arched tail.
"But I never write *anything*. If I print the name round
the figure on a vase, that's as far as *I* get."

"That's not what I mean. Your name is Alexis too. And
Great-grandfather was Leon, so that makes you 'Alexis son
of Leon' just as much as I am!"

"A most unfortunate coincidence."

"Coincidence my eye! It's the usual thing for an eldest
son to be named after his grandfather—Father was the eldest, so of course he had to be Leon."

"But I'm not *your* grandfather."

"No, but I'm not an eldest son, anyhow. Mother had me
named after you because she was sorry you hadn't any
grandchildren of your own."

"Your mother was a dear girl," said Uncle Paintbrush,
and he etched in another nymph, straight of nose and slender of ankle, a thumbnail portrait of his nephew's bride as
he first remembered her.

"Will you let me send it in under your name?" Alexis
begged. "It's only a matter of form. I don't suppose there's
one chance in a hundred that it'll be accepted."

"All right. I will—for her sake." With a deft squiggle he gave the nymph ringlets tumbling to her bare shoulders.

"Oh, *bless* you, Uncle Paintbrush!"

Alexis was so delighted he planted a kiss on the whiskery cheek, and the old man had to threaten him with a dab of black varnish before he could get on with his work.

12

And how long," inquired Milon smoothly, "should a good speech in the Assembly last?"

Alexis jerked himself back to life, realizing that the question was aimed at him. "Eight days, sir!" he said mechanically. There was an outburst of laughter from the other students. The old professor took a step toward him, his small eyes glinting unpleasantly.

"Indeed, Alexis? I venture to think that the audience would have grown a little weary—even of *your* well-known eloquence—by the end of that period."

The class cackled. "I—I'm sorry, sir. I must have been thinking of something else."

"So I should imagine. Perhaps we had better not inquire what. Well, let us continue, gentlemen. . . ."

Eight days, Alexis repeated to himself, eight days of waiting—and who knew when the suspense would end? Eight days ago the script had been sent in to the Minister Royal. Perhaps even at this moment that august official was sitting with the play unrolled upon his lap, his ancient dignity forgotten in sideshaking chuckles, while the other Festival entries lay ignored about his feet!

It was a pleasant daydream, but unlikely. The minister had other things to do besides judging playscripts. Was he not the second most important minister in the state? His very title, Minister Royal, dated from those far-off days when kings had ruled in Athens. Everything to do with public worship came under him, from a prosecution for atheism, such as Alexis had witnessed in court, to a religious festival. The spring festival of Dionysus was only one of these, and the choice of plays for it was only one part of the preparations.

Anyhow, Alexis told himself, what chance is there that he'll pick *The Gadfly*? He may have dozens to read, he can only choose three. Aristophanes is a certainty for one, he's so popular, he's won so often, the minister wouldn't dare to pass him over. . . . That leaves only two chances—

"So you see, gentlemen," Milon was droning on, "when you write out a speech beforehand, you will need to know how much to write for, say, one hour, two hours, or whatever time you wish to take. How many lines, roughly, would you write for an average speech before the Assembly? How many, Alexis?"

"Er—two, sir!" stammered Alexis, sitting up straight.

"H'm, two lines? A little brief, surely? You seem to have gone to the other extreme. Perhaps you will be good enough to compose and write out a speech and bring it to me tomorrow—not two lines, I think, but two hundred. Take as your subject 'that, in the opinion of this Assembly, the young should pay closer heed to the words of the old.'"

"Yes, sir," said Alexis, stifling a groan.

Day followed day. The suspense was cruel. It was worse because he had to bear it almost alone.

The family must not know he had sent in a play. He was
shy even of telling Lucian. Only two other living people
knew his secret: his great-uncle and Corinna. Uncle Paintbrush did not take the matter seriously at all; he had not
even read the script, and regarded the whole thing as a
boy's joke, to be humored and then forgotten. As for Corinna, there were not many chances of discussing it with
her. Gorgo had grown less welcoming of late, and, though
her kitchen was as warm as ever, her reception of Alexis
was chilly.

"He's no good to you, that boy," she grumbled to Corinna. "Gives you ideas above your class, talking to you as
if you was as good as him! I've no patience with it. Give
me a gentleman like Hippias, I know where I *am* with his
sort."

Do you? wondered Corinna, I'm not so sure. She remembered what Alex had told her. Hippias kept queer company
—men, like Magnes, who had been expelled from the city
and dared not show their faces by daylight. Her mother
might be sorry, some day, if she relied too much on Hippias.

"If you'd only do like he wants," Gorgo grumbled on,
"just go along with the others and play your flute at his
parties! You might do yourself some good—*and* me. You
might think of me sometimes, really you might, working
my fingers to the bone year in and year out, and you practically grown up, but still running wild like a little
kid——"

"I'm ready to work. Tell me what, and I'll do it."

"And keep upsetting the guests with your high and
mighty ways? No, thanks, I can get a slave girl to do the
jobs round the house, and do 'em better. Now if you took
up the flute serious, you could earn good money. You're
clever enough, you've had all sorts of advantages what *I've*
never had, and if you'd only learn to make yourself agree-

able to the right class, there'd be no stopping you. It makes me sick to see you wasting yourself, that's all."

Corinna shrugged her shoulders and made herself scarce. She hated the inn more and more. How different life would have been if she had had a father! Gorgo never said much about him, except that he had died when she was a baby. Gorgo was vague about most things in the past and you could hardly blame her, because she had been married three times and lived in so many different places that she got mixed up trying to remember them. Long ago Corinna had asked if she had ever had any brothers or sisters, and been told "no," she was the only one. Then, years later, when her mother was discussing babies with a neighbor, she heard her say, "Yes, I think of the time my boy was born, and the little fellow—" Corinna had questioned her afterward. "Then I did have a brother once! What happened, did he die?" Gorgo had looked at her startled for a moment. "Yes, dear, he died. I only had him a day or two. That's why I never talk about him much." "Oh, Mom, I *am* sorry!" she had said, tears starting to her eyes. It had helped her, afterward, to make allowances if Mom was hasty or rough. It must have been terrible losing a boy like that. Parents always wanted sons more than daughters.

She was reduced to meeting Alexis in the den, which was chilly now that winter had come and meant a long walk, often through rain and mud, but was better than not seeing each other at all. "If only we had a fire!" she said.

"Let's. Look, suppose I brought some live coals in a pot. There's loads of wood. If we collect some today and leave it here, we'll have it dry next time."

"And if I sneaked a few things from the kitchen, we could cook!"

"Oh, why didn't we think of it before?"

They got busy at once gathering up dead wood. The quarry echoed with the crack of branches snapped underfoot. That afternoon they were more carefree than they had been for weeks.

A few days later, as planned, Alexis brought up a pot with hot embers from the kitchen at home. "Nice!" sighed Corinna, pressing her cold hands round the warm earthenware. Then he carefully tipped out the embers on the dry cave floor, lay on his stomach and blew them gently into redness before feeding them with tiny twigs and fir cones. "*You* ought to do the blowing," he told her with a breathless chuckle.

"Why?"

"With all your flute playing, your wind should be better than mine!"

"I'm going to cook for you. Isn't that enough?"

"Depends on the cooking," he grunted.

The fire went better than he had dared to hope. He had half expected that there would be trouble over draft and that the cave would fill with clouds of smoke. But it seemed to lose itself in the shadowy interior, and in no time Corinna was cleaning the ashes from a heated stone and putting down dabs of muffin dough, which turned goldenbrown in a few moments and crumbled deliciously in the mouth.

"Happy?" she said when all the muffins were eaten, and they sat on either side of the dying fires hugging their knees.

"I'll say! If only I knew what was going to happen about the play. . . ."

"Would it help," she said slowly, "if I went to the temple of Dionysus tomorrow and made an offering? I couldn't give much, I'm afraid, and I don't dare ask Mom for anything, but——"

"Thanks, Corinna, but I don't think it'd help."

"Why not? He's the god of drama, it's *his* festival——"

"I didn't mean that. Of course, one should make offerings at the proper times. Socrates says so. But not just to beg special favors for oneself."

"That's what everybody *does*."

"Don't you see, though—if the gods exist they aren't like children, to be bribed with little presents? They're better than men, they're absolutely fair and just. So Dionysus will want to have the best plays chosen for his festival, not the ones whose authors spend most on sacrifices."

Corinna was only half convinced. She still felt that a little prayer and sacrifice would do no harm and might shorten this period of nerve-racking suspense. She decided that next morning, at sunrise, she would at least pour a little wine on the ground and whisper a private suggestion to Dionysus, to speed things up and not to miss one of the very best comedies ever submitted in his honor. Whether or not that did the trick, she was never quite sure, but by noon of that next day things had begun to happen.

"No, no, thank you, my dear, it's the boy I want—Alexis!"

The family was just finishing dinner when Uncle Paintbrush thrust a worried, whiskery face into the living room where they had meals during the cold weather. "Are you sure you've had your dinner?" Mother repeated with a smile.

"Yes, yes! I mean no. I mean, I don't want any dinner. I just want a word with Alexis, outside, if you don't mind."

Uncle Paintbrush looked extremely agitated. Alexis swung his legs off his couch. "Will you excuse me, Father?" he asked nervously.

Father gave him a sharp glance. "What's the boy been up to?" he demanded suspiciously.

Uncle Paintbrush pulled himself together with an effort.

"Nothing at all, Leon, nothing at all. Just want to talk to him. I—I want him to help me. Little bit of difficulty I'm in——"

"Can *I* help?"

"Oh, dear, no! Please don't trouble yourself, Leon. No, if I could just have the boy for a few minutes—perhaps I'd better have him for the whole afternoon——"

"Run along, then, Alexis," said Father with a smile. "See what you can do to help your great-uncle."

Outside, the old man groaned and said, "This is a fine thing you've let me in for. If I'd ever imagined for one moment——"

"What's the matter, Uncle? Is it—is it the play? Where are we going?" By this time they were in the street.

"We're going to see the Minister Royal!" announced the old man in the tone of one faced with utter disaster.

"The Minister Royal?" Alexis' heart leaped, then sank. "Does that mean . . . he's found out?"

"Heaven knows what it means! All I know is, a slave brought me a message, and the Minister Royal wants to see me. About my play. My play! And I've never even read it—much less written it! What on earth am I to say to him?" The vase painter's pale-blue eyes were panic-stricken.

"It depends on what he says to you, Uncle. You'll have to bluff for all you're worth."

"Bluff? Me bluff the Minister Royal?"

"I'll stand by you——"

"Very generous of you, my boy, very handsome!"

Alexis squeezed his arm affectionately. "If there's real trouble, you must blame it all on me. I'll own up to everything."

"Well, we'll see, we'll see." Uncle Paintbrush had begun to recover a little of his nerve. "No need to start talking about that till we've heard what he says . . . yes, you're

right there. I'll take my cue from him." He chuckled. "You
see, I'm practicing theater talk already—'take my cue,'
that's right, isn't it?"

"You're a sport, Uncle," Alexis assured him with a laugh.

Uncle Paintbrush preened himself. "We shall have to decide what sort of an act we are going to put on," he said.
"Listen to me! 'Put on an act,' now! It's quite easy to fall
into the right way of speaking, isn't it?"

"Yes, but I wouldn't overdo it."

They were now within sight of the hall where the Minister Royal and his committees carried out their official
business. Hastily they decided on a plan of action.

The minister was elderly, with a hint of humor in his eye.
He stood up to greet them. "Alexis Leonides?" he inquired.

"Yes, Minister." Uncle Paintbrush answered with respect
but also with dignity. He did not bow, for the minister was
only a citizen like himself, elected for a year.

"Sit down, then. Who is the boy?"

"My grandnephew. He—he helps me in various ways."
Uncle Paintbrush sat down opposite the minister, and
Alexis stood beside him, his eyes narrowed and wary.

"I must confess," said the minister, stroking his beard,
"I had expected, after reading the play, to see someone
rather younger."

"*Younger?*" echoed the old vase painter. "Oh, I see!
Younger than me, you mean."

"Of course! Forgive me—I know age is no bar to good
writing. Look at Sophocles, turning out great tragedies at
ninety! But he *started* young. You seem a little elderly,
Alexis, to be entering the Festival for the first time."

"A man's as young as he feels, Minister."

The minister's eyes twinkled. "And you, apparently, feel
very sprightly indeed. I really must congratulate you. *The
Gadfly* reads more like the work of a twenty-year-old."

"Oh, I'm not such a back number as you might think."

"Anything but, my dear sir! Well," the minister continued more seriously, "I've been wondering very much whether to accept your play or not. It has its faults, of course——"

"Granted," said the old man, rather too readily, in the boy's opinion.

"Though it also has distinct merits."

"I'm glad to hear you say so." Alexis, standing rigid beside his great-uncle, hoped that the minister would not raise his eyes and notice the pinkness in his cheeks.

"One or two production difficulties occurred to me as I read it. How are you going to get a cow on the stage?"

"A *cow?*" the old vase painter echoed blankly.

"You remember, Uncle," Alexis prompted him hastily, "that broad comedy scene where the cow is stung by the gadfly and goes cavorting all over the place!"

"Yes," said the minister, "how are you going to do that?"

Uncle Paintbrush hesitated. The anxious look crept back into his eyes. As he fingered his whisker and mumbled, Alexis said quickly, "I think, sir, Uncle meant to use two men inside a big spotty skin—the front one with a mask and horns, and the back one with a tail, and so forth——"

"That's the idea," said Uncle Paintbrush quickly. "Get a good laugh, that would."

"H'm. . . . You think it would work?"

"Why not, sir?" Alexis demanded warmly. "Someone used a centaur the year before last—*that* was two men in a skin."

"Did they?" inquired the minister, shooting him a keen glance. "I missed that festival, I was away with the fleet. H'm." He pondered, stroking his beard. Alexis held his breath. Was it possible to fool this man? Those kindly eyes were shrewd. No doubt they could be stern too. They were

trained to see through the lies of politicians and foreign
ambassadors. What chance against them had he and Uncle
Paintbrush? For a few moments he felt almost paralyzed
by his own impudence. He wished they had confessed the
truth at first, for it was too late now. But if they had, it
would have been good-by to any chance of seeing the play
produced. No minister, whatever his personal opinion,
would have dared to insult the Athenian public by offering
them a play written by a mere boy.

Suddenly the minister raised his head and addressed the
vase painter again. "Another difficulty occurred to me," he
said slowly. "The entrance of the Egyptian slave, in the
third episode."

"Oh . . . well . . ." began Uncle Paintbrush. "Of
course——"

"But, Uncle, surely the minister is mixing up your play
with one of the others?" Alexis bent forward with an in-
tense and meaning scowl, his words loaded with warning.
"There *is* no Egyptian slave in yours. Er—is there?"

"Of course not," said Uncle Paintbrush almost irritably,
"that's what I was just going to say. There is no Egyptian
slave in the play. You took the words out of my mouth."

"I apologize," said the minister smoothly. "It is easy to
get confused when one has read several dozen plays." He
looked up and gave Alexis a long, level stare. "Your nephew
must be a great help. He seems to know your play almost
as well as you do."

"I wrote out most of it for him, sir," said Alexis demurely. "Uncle's eyes aren't what they were."

"Well," said the minister, "there are other questions I
would like to ask, but I think on the whole it would be better if I did not." He stood up to show that the interview
was over. "You understand, both of you, it is nothing to
me whether a playwright is as old as the hills, or——" he
added with a flicker of a smile toward the boy "as young

as . . . well, as young as you like. But I have my duty
to the Athenian public, and, as you know, they are very
easily offended."

"Oh, we quite understand," said Uncle Paintbrush affa-
bly, though he had not the faintest idea whether the play
was accepted or not.

Alexis moistened his lips. "Does that mean, sir," he ven-
tured with a gulp, "that—that it's no good? The play's
out?"

"Certainly not, my boy. It is well worth producing. I
know of no reason why it should not be produced—and I
may add—" again that smile flickered across his face—"I
do not *wish* to know of any reason." He turned to Uncle
Paintbrush, whose features were contorted with amazement
and alarm. "You will be told the name of your financial
backer and the cast I allot you. I pay their salaries, but
your backer will pay the chorus and all other expenses.
You, of course, will be responsible for the actual production——"

"Me? But, heavens——"

"You may act a part too, if you wish it," said the minister pleasantly. "I expect your nephew will be a great help
to you at rehearsals. He will be able to remember things
which you yourself forget, and I have no doubt he will be
most ingenious at overcoming difficulties."

"But, my dear Minister——"

"Good luck, my dear sir. And—good afternoon."

They found themselves alone, and outside.

13

For the second time that afternoon the elder Alexis faced the younger and exclaimed in broken accents, "This is a fine thing you've let me in for!"

The boy almost danced round him. "But, Uncle, it's wonderful! Don't you realize he's accepted it? My play! It's to be done at the Festival! Would you mind pinching me, just to make sure I'm awake?"

"I'd like to do more than pinch you." Uncle Paintbrush scratched his head. "What on earth do we do now?"

"Go ahead! Produce the play!"

"Talk sense, boy. How can we? I don't know the first thing about it."

"But *I* do."

"Then you'd better get on with it." Uncle Paintbrush stumped away, banging his staff at every other step to relieve his feelings. Alexis ran after him and began to coax him.

"But, Uncle, the actors won't take any notice of a boy——"

"No, they've more sense than I have."

"You can't let me down now! Listen, I'll tell you what to say. All you've got to do is to say it."

"I'll be the laughingstock of Athens," grumbled the old man. "I can hear the gossip already! 'Fancy *him* writing a play! When are you going to write another one?' My whole life will be changed! I've always been a quiet sort of fellow, going along in my own little way, and now it'll all be spoiled. I shall have to act a part for the rest of my life."

"Only till the Festival! Once it's safely over, and they've agreed the play was all right, we can let the secret out and you won't be bothered any more."

"*If* the play's all right! But if it's a failure, we'll have to keep quiet still, for the sake of the minister."

Alexis nodded, feeling rather ashamed. "It *is* pretty much a case of 'heads I win, tails you lose,' " he admitted.

Uncle Paintbrush stopped in his tracks, banged his staff on the ground, and said with unusual firmness, "I'm going back. I'm going to explain everything."

"Then the play will never be done!"

"You can send it in yourself in a few years' time." Uncle Paintbrush turned and began to march back. Alexis ran after him again, tugging at his cloak.

"That'll be no good," he implored him. "It's topical. It must be done this year."

"Can't help that!" Uncle Paintbrush puffed out his cheeks and strode on, very red.

Alexis tried one last appeal. "Mother will be so disappointed. . . ." His uncle stopped.

"Your mother? Why?"

"Well, she'd be thrilled to know I'd written a play good enough to be accepted—but she'd be pretty sick if she heard now that you'd wrecked everything when it was all decided."

Uncle Paintbrush pondered for a moment, turned yet

again, banged his staff harder than ever on the ground, and resumed his homeward march. "You're much too much like your mother," he growled.

"How?"

"*She* could always twist me around her little finger too."

They agreed on their way home that the secret should be kept from the family for the time being. "Not that I like acting a part to your mother and father," the old man grumbled, "But there's one thing that'd make me feel even worse."

"What's that?"

"Acting the part to everybody else, and knowing your mother and father were watching me all the time!"

So he had to submit, with as good grace as possible, to the amazed congratulations of his relatives and neighbors.

"Well, Uncle, I can hardly believe it," said Father.

"I always knew there was a lot in Uncle Paintbrush you others couldn't appreciate," said Mother wisely.

"Clever Uncle Paintbrush!" chanted Theo, dancing round excitedly. "You'll let me go behind the scenes, won't you?"

"*I* won't even see it from the front," Nico grumbled.

"We are all very proud, sir," Parmeno murmured to him, with the freedom of an old family slave.

Uncle Paintbrush was somewhat bewildered by the congratulations and questions showered upon him, but he remembered to ask Father if Alexis could be let off classes, when necessary, to help him at rehearsals. Father could not very well refuse, and Alexis made a private resolution that it would be "necessary" every day.

It was a little galling to hear so many congratulations heaped upon Uncle Paintbrush which should by rights have been his. Uncle Paintbrush was loving it, once he had grown accustomed to his part. After being held up as the failure of the family for about seventy years, he enjoyed the new sensation of glory. Alexis left him to it, and almost ran to the inn. He just had to tell the news to someone who knew the truth.

Corinna was coming through the archway, an empty water jar on her head. She almost dropped it when he clutched her hands and stammered out his story. "Oh, Alex! How *marvelous!*" Her whole face lit up. Then she glanced round. "Walk to the fountain with me. You know what Mom is. Oh, I *am* glad. And I do think your old uncle is a dear."

"He's a scream. Half the time he's scared stiff, then he has a little burst of confidence and really enjoys pretending he's a playwright. Heaven knows how we'll pull through all the rehearsals without *somebody* finding out!"

They reached the fountain. She put the jar under the lion-head spout. The crystal water gushed in with a hollow rumble. Then, with a graceful twirl of her arms, she set the jar on her head again, straightened her back, and turned to go. "I wish *I* could do something to help," she said.

"You've helped a lot already," he assured her. "I don't think I'd ever have finished the play but for you."

The next day it was publicly announced that the Festival plays were those sent in by Aristophanes, Eupolis, and Alexis. Each author was allotted a *choregus*, or backer. This kind of burden fell upon every wealthy taxpayer sooner or later: if it was not a play he had to finance, it was a warship.

A man named Conon was to pay the expenses of *The Gadfly*. Uncle Paintbrush made a face when he heard. "What's the matter?" Alexis demanded. "Anything wrong with him?"

"No-no, my boy, but I'd rather have had someone else."

"Why?"

"Well . . ." Uncle Paintbrush hesitated, scratching his head. "I don't know quite how to put it. But Conon's not a *happy* man. He very seldom comes into the town—I don't think he's been to the theater for years———"

"Oh." Alexis made a face. Conon did not sound likely to prove an enthusiastic supporter. "Where does he live?"

"He has a farm out beyond Colonus. Spends all his time there. They say he lives as simply as a peasant—though he must have plenty of money. Owns a silver mine."

"Do you mean he's a miser?"

"I wouldn't say that, my boy. He was openhanded enough in the old days, I believe. But of late he's shut himself up in the country and everyone's lost sight of him. Except," Uncle Paintbrush added with a chuckle, "the tax collector."

"Sounds like a mystery man! Will we have to go out and see him?"

"Well, he certainly won't come into the city to see *us*."

So that afternoon the vases were left unpainted and the pair set out through the pale sunshine. It was one of those clean, crisp winter days, when the bare trees stood out against blue sky and snow-sprinkled mountains, and the white gulls circled, harshly crying, above the furrows.

They passed a small shrine, walked through a woodland famous in summer for its nightingales, and spoke to a man ploughing. "Conon?" he echoed, and jerked his thumb. "Follow that track—the one that goes to the Theban border. You'll find his farm a half mile on. Though whether you'll find the old man in or not . . . or what kind of welcome you'll meet with—however, good luck to you!"

"Sounds as though we'll need it," Alexis murmured.

It seemed a long half mile. Uncle Paintbrush paused, breathless, leaning heavily on his staff. He remembered that there were two paths from Colonus to the Theban frontier. Had the ploughman meant the other one? "Listen," said

Alexis, "there's someone riding up behind. We can ask him."

The drumming of hoofs grew louder. The horseman arrived suddenly on the crest of a steep bank above the path and reined in, as though surprised to see them. He made a striking picture against the blue sky and scurrying cloud—a gaunt figure with a face which might have been hacked from rock, astride a gray stallion compounded of marble and silk and fire. Alexis caught his breath sharply. It was as though Poseidon himself, the horsebreaking god, had risen from a crack in the earth.

The stranger looked as though he would have wheeled and ridden away, but at Uncle Paintbrush's shout he plunged recklessly down the bank and came to a standstill in front of them.

"Wasn't that rather dangerous?" said Uncle Paintbrush.

The rider stared at him sharply and apparently decided that he was old enough to say what he liked. He laughed shortly. "If you don't care about death, nothing happens to you. Or so I've found. Have you lost your way?"

"I'm not altogether sure," said Uncle Paintbrush. "We want Conon's farm——"

"I'm Conon." Alexis stared with increased interest at the rider. He was not as old as Uncle Paintbrush, but much older than Father. His skin, close up, was leathery and deeply lined. He must have been good-looking long ago. There was still a sort of ruinous magnificence about him. "I'm Conon," he repeated, his tone curter than ever. They began to explain. "I know, I know," he interrupted. "I had the message from the Minister Royal this morning. How much do you want?"

"Well—er—you see——"

"It's rather a question, sir," Alexis interrupted boldly, "of how much we can have."

Conon looked at him properly for the first time. His tone

softened ever so slightly. "And who may you be? Not a son—at your age?" He shot an inquiring glance at Uncle Paintbrush.

"Oh, no," said the vase painter hurriedly. "I was never even married. So, to my sorrow, I've never had a son."

"Count yourself lucky. Your sorrow might have been greater," said Conon heavily. There was an awkward pause.

"He's my great-nephew," said Uncle Paintbrush all in a nervous rush. "He's helping me with the production—he's really extremely clever—I brought him along because he has a better head for details—I can't remember things as well as I used to——"

"That too may not be such a misfortune as you imagine," said Conon, but it was clear to Alexis that his mind was on something else. Then, seeming to pull himself together, he added, "Well, you've had a good walk. You'd better come into the house and sit down, and we'll settle whatever's necessary."

He turned his horse, and they walked beside him. To relieve the strained silence Alexis made an admiring remark about the stallion, and Conon, in his grim way, seemed pleased. "Couldn't live at Colonus without breeding horses, you know. After all, they say that horses were first tamed here, and the village gets its name from the man who did it."

The farmhouse was biggish, beautifully set on the south side of a craggy hillock. A great walnut tree shadowed it, there was an orchard of gnarled old apple trees, and withered vines trailed over a trellis which must have made a delightful shelter a month or two before. Most of all Alexis liked the stream which came spurting and swirling down its rocky channel.

Conon slid from his horse, handed the bridle to a surprised-looking slave, and led the way into a living room warmed by a small charcoal brazier. A graceful elderly lady rose silently, gathered up her embroidery, and prepared to go, but Conon checked her with a gesture. "No need to go, my dear," he said gently. He turned to Uncle Paintbrush. "My wife, Demetria," he explained. "We live a simple life out here—we don't stand on all the conventions of the city. Never could see why the lady of the house should scuttle out of her own living room like a rabbit every time her husband brings in a visitor!"

"But I will just get our friends some refreshment," said Demetria in a low voice, smiling faintly, and she vanished, to return in a few moments with a maid carrying wine and cakes.

"Bless my soul—one of my wine jars!" cried Uncle Paintbrush, as delighted as a small child, and everyone stopped to admire the delicate figures he remembered painting nearly twenty years before.

"We live simply," said Demetria, sitting down again, "but what we have, my husband likes to be the very best."

Gracefully put, thought Alexis. He looked at his uncle, comfortably seated with a cushion for his old bones, purring with satisfaction. Then he caught Demetria's calm gray eye.

"You must have another cake," she insisted. "How old are you?" He told her. "Really? Our child would have been nearly as old within a few months. . . ." She sighed, and bent over her embroidery.

"Our visitors have come to talk about the Festival," said Conon in a harsher tone than he had used since entering the house. "Now, sir, can you tell me the extent of my responsibilities? I haven't taken much interest in the theater of late years, but I'm quite ready to do the proper thing."

"Thank you. I'm sure you can't speak fairer than that." The old man turned appealingly to the boy. "Er—I got my great-nephew here to jot down the main points."

"Here you are, sir." Alexis drew a list from the folds of his tunic. "Twenty-four men in the chorus, with extra pay for the leader. One flute player. You don't have to worry about the three principals, because the minister pays them. We've been lucky in the draw, we've got three good actors, Dio and——"

"I'm afraid the names won't mean anything to me," said Conon briskly. "I can't say how long it is since I saw a play."

"Six years," interrupted his wife impulsively, "you know it is six years since——"

"Get on with your list!" Conon ordered, his face darkening. Alexis went on obediently.

"Apart from their wages, sir, there'll be costumes. I thought—I mean, my uncle thought—we'd have everything as gay as possible. Plenty of color. They'll need tunics, cloaks, tights, shoes, masks, body padding for the comic fat ones. . . . Then there's a special costume needed for the name part, and we have a 'cow' with two men inside——"

"How are you going to get hold of that?"

"Oh, there are workmen who specialize in masks and theater properties, sir. I know just where to go."

"Is that the whole list?"

"The main items, sir. Sure to be extras later."

"Yes, he's remembered everything I told him," said Uncle Paintbrush, feeling he had been too long in the background.

"What will that come to—roughly?"

Alexis named a figure, eyeing him rather nervously as he did so. To his relief, Conon answered, "That's not very much. Don't stint yourselves. Do the job properly."

"You're very generous, sir," said Uncle Paintbrush.

"Can't take my money to the grave with me, can I? What use is it to me?" Conon growled. "I'll tell my banker to keep you supplied. If there's anything else you want, let me know."

They all stood up. Conon laid his hand on the boy's shoulder, saying to Uncle Paintbrush, "You'll be busy, no doubt, and it's a tidy step out here. Send the boy if you like. Always glad to see him."

"Thank you," said Uncle Paintbrush, much relieved, "it might be more convenient, certainly."

It was sunset as Conon saw them off, pointing out a short cut across the fields. The whole western sky was aflame. Fir tree and cypress and distant mountain range stood up black against the red.

"Not a bad old fellow, when you get to know him," Alexis commented when they were out of hearing.

"I'm trying to remember what it was I heard about him in his younger days," murmured the old man. "Yes, now I've seen his wife, I think he *would* be the one. . . ."

"Which one?"

"There was a Conon who caused quite a sensation, marrying a woman nearly as old as himself, instead of a young girl. . . . They were both nearly thirty at the time. It was a real love match, not the usual thing arranged between families."

"Did they have any children?"

"N-no. . . . At least, not for a long time. I'm sure of that, because it was a great grief to them. I don't know about later on."

"I think they must have had," said Alexis, "from the way they both talked."

"I really couldn't say." Uncle Paintbrush groaned as his old limbs began to protest again all this unusual excercise. But as they drew near the pathway Alexis found his answer. A simple marble tomb gleamed whitely in the twilight under a clump of firs. He was just able to spell out the verses engraved upon it:

Pause, stranger, where I lie, Lycomedes,
Old Conon's only son, beneath the trees.
For nine sweet years I ranged o'er field and hill,
And now, the brief race run, my feet are still.

"I remember now," mumbled Uncle Paintbrush. "He died of fever. Comes back to me now. Very sad. People said it showed how silly he'd been to marry a wife nearly his own age."

"Why?"

"Because, stupid, it was obvious she'd never have any more children to take the boy's place."

Alexis walked on without speaking for some time. He knew now why it was six years since Conon had been to the theater.

Rehearsal began a few days later, as soon as the actors had copies of their parts and the two dozen men dancers had been engaged for the chorus. This, Alexis found, was his worst worry. The actors were experienced professionals, and could be relied on to deliver their lines to good effect and to invent plenty of comic "business" of their own. There were only the three of them, dividing the seven speaking parts—the junior man "doubled" no fewer than four small characters—so there were no awkward problems of grouping for a producer to solve. The only thing to do with the actors was to give them their heads and hope for the best.

With the chorus it was different. Their slow, formal movements—the way they divided and reformed and marched in procession—called for the precision of a drill display. The flute player would keep them in time, but everything else depended on the producer. Alexis soon realized that it would take something like strict military discipline to get those dances right. Uncle Paintbrush could never apply that. Nor could he. The very first rehearsal made it all too painfully clear. The dancers turned mulish. They laughed behind their hands, and their leader, a man named Glaucus, was openly rude to Uncle Paintbrush.

Alexis was in despair. Then he saw that there was only one thing to do. Glaucus must somehow be changed from the ringleader of the rebels into an ally. He was not an attractive person, but Alexis had to see his point of view. He knew his own job as head man in the chorus and did not like being ordered about by a beginner.

Alexis approached him after rehearsal. "You must make allowances for Uncle," he murmured, "he's very old, you know."

"Too old to start play producing at his time of life," said Glaucus frankly. "It beats me how he ever wrote the thing. The play itself is *good*, but he doesn't know the first thing about drilling a chorus. Trouble with these old fellows is, you can't tell 'em anything."

"I know," said Alexis cunningly, "it must be maddening for anyone who's been in lots of plays as you have and really knows what's what. I say, Glaucus, I have an idea!"

"What's that?"

"He'll listen to *me*, you know. Suppose you and I got together, and you told me what you thought about the dances? Then I'd talk to my uncle—and I bet I could make him think the ideas were his own!"

Glaucus laughed. "You're a crafty one," he said.

How crafty, he did not realize. For Alexis was able at the same time to pick the dancer's brains and slip in his own ideas as well, so that Glaucus could not see the difference. Uncle Paintbrush was planted in a seat as far back from the stage as possible, where he signaled angrily if he could not hear the lines spoken. To save his legs, he used his nimble nephew as messenger between himself and the cast, and Alexis was able to deliver his own instructions as though they had come from the figure huddled at the back.

Glaucus practically ran the chorus at all later rehearsals, and there was no more revolt. It was not going to be a brilliantly original production, Alexis told himself, but at least it would be competent and professional. The play would have to stand or fall on the merits of the script he had written. So be it!

There was not much time for seeing Corinna nowadays, but she was eager to know how things were going, and at last they managed to meet outside the city and go up to the cave. The snow had come down to the plain by now and they were glad of the earthen jar, warm from the embers inside, which they took turns to carry. "Brrh!" said Corinna, shuddering. "Thank heaven it'll soon be spring!"

"Spring's coming far too fast! Only ten days to the Festival, and the play isn't nearly ready."

She had to hear everything in detail, from the first visit to Conon's farm—she thought that he and it and Demetria all sounded delightful—to the very last argument Glaucus had had with the flute player, and what the men at the shop had said when they were asked to build a comical cow.

"How exciting it all is!" she exclaimed. "Lucky Alex, you get all the excitement, and I never——"

"Sh!" He checked her, his hand on her arm. They had picked their way across the swollen river, where snow-encrusted boulders rose from icy green water, and they were standing at the mouth of the quarry. "Someone's been to the den!"

A double set of footprints wound their way through the oleander bushes to the foot of the rock.

"There's no one there now," she pointed out. "You can see it was only one man—the marks go in and come out again. And they were made before yesterday's snowfall."

"Yes, they're half blotted out, aren't they?"

"Come on, then. Anyhow, nobody's going to keep us out of our cave." They hurried across the quarry and clambered up into the cleft. "Some nerve!" she snorted. "He lit a fire, too. But he didn't find our wood supply. He had to use damp stuff, and it didn't all burn." She kicked aside the charred twigs contemptuously.

"Say!" Alexis exclaimed. "What's this?" He stooped and picked up from the fragments a long thin strip of scorched cloth, no wider than his thumbnail. "There's writing on it."

Looking over his shoulder she read the letters aloud: "F P A B E E E P I L R—" She stopped impatiently. "What's the sense of it? It doesn't *mean* anything."

"It must," he said. "But what?"

14

I know what this thing is," said Alexis excitedly.

"It's a *skytaly*!"

"A how much?"

"A stick message! It's a dodge the Spartans use for sending secret dispatches."

"How does it work?"

"They twist parchment—or cloth in this case—round a stick. Round and round like a bandage. Then they write the message along the *length* of the stick, so that when it's unrolled you just get a jumble of single letters, like this."

"And you can only read it if you wind it on the stick again!"

"Smart girl! The same stick, or one the same diameter."

Her face fell. "We've no idea what size stick was used for this message." She looked despairingly at the strip of cloth in her hand with its scrawled characters.

FPABEEEPILREAHOPNAEMTOFIANTATUHALSODHSIS.

139

Alexis was poking round the cave in the dim light which crept through the entrance. "Seems to have spent the night here, whoever he was. Brought in a lot of leaves and ferns to sleep on. He's left his old eggshells too, and this meat bone."

"I like his nerve! *Our* cave. . . . Say, Alex, do you think he was a Spartan spy?"

"I don't know. Must have been something queer about him, or why should he sleep up here, when the city's only a few miles away—and houses much nearer than that?"

"If only we could read that message!"

"You know, I think we *could*. With patience."

"Oh, dear!" She scrambled to her feet. "Is this where we sally forth and gather sticks—thick sticks and thin sticks, wands, cudgels, tree trunks——"

"No, idiot! It can be done without any sticks at all. Just common sense. It's a childishly simple code, really; only those thickheaded Spartans would think it clever."

"I'm afraid I'm a thickheaded Spartan," she said meekly.

"You're not. Now think."

"I'm thinking."

He picked up a thickish branch at random and wound the cloth round twice. "This is only an example," he said. "Let's see how many letters it takes to go once around the stick. Seven. So if this *were* the right stick, we'd have the eighth letter following the first, and then the fifteenth——"

"FPO—not a very bright beginning!"

"Which shows that seven isn't the number, unless there's a double trick in the code. Now, with letters written this size, the number wouldn't be two, three or four——"

"It would mean such an impossibly thin stick?"

"Exactly. I bet it's more than five, and less than twelve, or it *would* have to be wound around a treetrunk."

"Then," she cried, her eyes dancing, "we only have to

try out a few different ways, till one of them makes sense!"

He nodded. "We know it isn't every seventh letter. You try the numbers below seven, and I'll do eight and over."

They held the strip of cloth between them, mumbling over it as though casting some mysterious spell. Almost immediately Alexis let out a cry.

"Quiet!" she protested. "You've made me lose count."

"Never mind. I've got it. It's eight. Look." He took a sharp twig and scratched the letters on a sandy patch in the cave mouth.

```
F P A B E E E P
I L R E A H O P
N A E M T O F I
A N T A T U H A
L S O D H S I S
```

"Hippias!" she cried.

"Yes," he said soberly, reading the columns downward: " 'Final plans are to be made at the house of Hippias. . . .' "

"Plans for what?"

"That's what we've got to find out."

All the suspicions which had worried Alexis months ago now sprang to life again. Surely their find linked up with the stranger he had seen at the torch race, and with the portrait statue in Cephalus' studio?

"It's some sort of a plot," he insisted. "Hippias is in league with Magnes. Magnes was last heard of in Sparta— this is a Spartan code method. Don't you see how it all ties up? The man who used the cave was either Magnes or some messenger passing between him and Hippias. I don't like the sound of 'final plans.' They must be getting ready to do something drastic."

"A revolution?"

He nodded. "It's been tried before. They'd overthrow

the democratic government, and bring back Magnes, I suppose, as a kind of dictator. I don't see how they'd do it. But perhaps the Spartans would lend a hand. It would suit Sparta to wipe out our democracy."

"Who can we tell?" asked Corinna sensibly.

"That's the trouble." He played with the strip of cloth, irritably. "This is our only fresh evidence. Not much, is it? Lucian told his uncle last time, but the Council pooh-poohed the idea. We need something more definite before we go running to them again."

"Are you going to tell Lucian?"

"I think I ought to, don't you? He was in it with me before. I don't know what he'll say."

"I know one thing he'll say," she grumbled, " 'Keep that girl out, we don't want *her* mixed up in it.' "

"Oh, I don't know," said Alexis weakly. But he did.

"I don't see what you and Lucian can do that you didn't do before," she argued. "You both trailed around after Hippias, but you never found out anything. If there's any evidence to be picked up it's no good looking in the streets. It'll be where this message says, in his house. How will you get at it there?"

"We might—we might break in. . . . Or something . . ."

"Or something!" she jeered. "And the girl who can walk in openly, with no suspicions aroused—*she's* no good, *she's* to be kept out of everything!"

"What do you mean?"

"Hippias is giving another big party next week, a few days before the Festival. Judging by the list of guests, he's asking all his political cronies. I don't suppose he's timing his revolution *before* then—more likely the party's a cover for them to get together and make these 'final plans'——"

"Say! If I could get into the house, I might hide and listen——"

"Don't be a child, Alex," she interrupted roughly. "This

isn't a game. Do you think they won't take precautions? Of course, if you *want* your throat cut . . . ! There'll be no uninvited guests that evening. If it is the plotters' final rally, they'll want to know every man who crosses the threshold. No, don't you see, the only people they won't bother about will be the *girls*, the poor dumb females who're fit for nothing but to dance and throw roses about. And," she added meaningly, "to play the flute."

"*What?*" cried Alexis aghast. "You don't mean you'd——"

"In a good cause," she said firmly. "Don't look so worried. I can take care of myself." She gave one of her silent laughs. "If the party gets lively I shall chew garlic—if anyone tries to kiss me, he won't do it again."

"But——" Alexis was still unhappy at the thought, though the vision of an oniony Corinna repelling unwanted embraces had its comic side. He groped for some argument against the scheme. "If it is the evening the plotters meet," he suggested, "it won't be that sort of party."

"It'll be made to *look* like that sort of party," she retorted. "Hippias never has any kind of banquet without plenty of song and dance. It would look pretty suspicious if he cut all that out, this time. I bet there'll be more fun and games than ever, if only to drown the noise of the plotters muttering away in the corner. Anyhow, he came to see Mom a few days ago and ordered all the usual." She stood up, brushing her dress. "Come on, or we'll have to cross the river in the dark. I'm going straight home to say I've changed my mind and I'm going out as a flute girl!" She shook with inward amusement. "*Won't* Mom be pleased?"

Some of her self-confidence faded as the week went by. She hated the thought of showing herself off as a public entertainer. Sometimes she went hot and cold, imagining the crowd of guests, the way they would stare and pass personal comments without troubling to lower their voices. She had not spent her whole childhood in common taverns without learning something of life, and her whole nature revolted against the uglier side of it.

Only her pride stopped her from backing out. She would go through with the plan, she told herself, but, oh! how glad she would be when it was over. Would the week never pass?

Alexis was lucky. He had other things to occupy his mind. His play was in the last frenzied fortnight of rehearsal. He was flying about from the theater to the mask maker's shop, he was routing out Uncle Paintbrush from the pottery where he sometimes took refuge, he was tramping out to Conon's farm—for Conon was taking an unexpected interest in the production and demanded up-to-date bulletins of its progress. Corinna scarcely saw him, and then only for two or three brief snatched conversations. She said, half jokingly, "You authors! You might think nothing in the world mattered except the play. I'm the one who has to remember the state's in danger!"

Alexis blinked. Then he smiled. "Sorry. You're quite right—in a way. It's a funny thing, how terribly important one's work becomes—to oneself. You know, when we first read that code message, can you guess the thought that leaped into my mind?"

She laughed. "I think so. 'Merciful gods, no revolution till after the play's over—*please!*'"

"Yes. I was afraid so: you know me much too well!"

"You can't help it. That's what being an author means."

"It makes one feel horribly selfish," he said ruefully. "In the same way, I started the play because I wanted to help Socrates. Now I forget about that for whole days together. I only think about making the play a success."

"Why not? The better it goes, the more it'll help him."

"I hope so," he said earnestly. "I couldn't bear anything to happen to him. He's in worse danger than ever, with this other trouble brewing."

"Why?"

"Because he won't take sides. He criticizes the democrats when he thinks *they're* wrong, and he criticizes the other side too. Instead of everybody saying how fair-minded he is, they all regard him as a dangerous nuisance. If it comes to fighting—" He broke off, unwilling to finish his own thought. He had heard enough about revolutions to know that in such times civilization was apt to break down, even among Greeks.

Two days later came Hippias' party. It was held in the biggish house, close to the Areopagus hill, which he had inherited from his aristocratic father.

Corinna had high words with her mother when she was getting ready. "I'm not going to wear *that*," she said flatly when her new dress was produced.

"But it's the best Coan stuff," Gorgo protested, letting it flow and shimmer through her work-worn fingers. "Light as gossamer, it is."

"It's a darned sight *too* light," Corinna retorted, sticking out her small chin obstinately. "No, thanks, I might as well dress in water—or air."

"Well, if you want to go like an old frump! I'd have given my eyes for stuff like this at your age. All the dancers'll be wearing it. But you always have to be different."

There was another argument over the make-up. Corinna had quite enjoyed having her dark hair curled and dressed in an older, more elaborate style than usual, and she did not refuse her mother's dabs of perfume from the alabaster bottle, though she smiled to herself at the thought of her secret store of garlic leaves. But when it came to rubbing white lead into her already creamy skin, to reddening her

cheeks with rouge, and darkening her eyebrows with lamp-
black, as the other girls did, she put her foot down.

"You wouldn't like me to dye my hair, would you?" she
demanded with heavy sarcasm. "Or add on a few yards of
somebody else's?"

"Of course not, dear! You have a lovely head of hair—
you don't want any false additions, nor dyes either. But I
do wish you'd let me touch up your eyes a tiny bit, and
your cheeks maybe——"

"I'm a girl, Mom, not a new war galley you're launch-
ing!"

"I only want you to do yourself justice," said Gorgo sor-
rowfully. "You'll look so pale and washed-out beside the
others—it'll be lamplight, remember. You'll hardly be noticed."

So much the better, Corinna said to herself. Aloud, to
console her disappointed parent, she said with youthful
frankness, "It's be no good, Mom. I get so hot, playing for
a long time, especially in a crowd. I would only perspire,
and then I'd be a fine sight with all that stuff streaking
down my face."

In the end Gorgo agreed to let the natural bloom of maid-
enhood go unassisted, and when the troupe set off for Hippias', Corinna went in her best saffron-yellow dress without
any of the artificial aids to face and figure adopted by the
older girls.

15

The party was going well, as parties did when Gorgo presided behind the scenes. The low ornamental tables had been removed with the remnants of chicken and pheasant and quail, shellfish and eels and other delicacies, garnished with all the skill she had learned in Syracuse. The floor had been swept of scraps, slaves had carried round water for hand-washing, and now the tables were set again between the couches, laden with fruit and salted almonds, sweets and cheese. In came the wines, red, white, and yellow, and pure water to mix with them in the great bowls.

Hippias stood amid his guests, goblet in hand, ready to pour the first few drops upon the floor in honor of the gods. Peeping through the open doorway, Corinna thought he looked well-satisfied with the evening and with himself. His long hair looked as though it were fresh, like her own, from the curling irons. His rings flashed in the lamplight as he made elegant gestures of command.

"Music, out there!" he called, and obediently she set the double flute to her lips, and all the men in the room joined in the old chant which opened the second half of the evening. As the last notes died away, Hippias cried out, "Good health!" and poured the offering to the gods. Then, cutting across the babble of talk, he demanded, "Now, gentlemen, whom do you choose as Master of Cermonies?"

There was a chorus of "Hippias!" Flushing with pleasure, the young man answered, "If you insist! Then I rule we drink three-and-two tonight—three parts water, two of wine, that is—and we'll start with the red Chian. Agreed? Pass round the cups, and let's have some music!"

"That's our cue, dearie," said a husky voice in Corinna's ear. "Here we go, girls!"

This time the flute plunged into a lively tune. Corinna stood in the doorway while one by one the dancers shimmered past her in the filmy draperies. Then, with a certain fluttering of her own—but deep down in her stomach—she followed.

The big dining room was hot after the frosty air of the courtyard. Some of the guests had pushed their robes off their shoulders, and leaned on their elbows, bare and glistening to the waist, red-faced, the garlands already limp and wilting on their brows.

So these, she thought as she slipped into a corner and made herself as small as possible, were "the best people"! She had plenty of leisure to look around. The flute was not needed all the time, and in any case there were breaks in the entertainment while the wine cups were refilled. As the evening wore on these breaks grew longer. Some of the guests seemed to prefer talking to the dancers instead of watching them. Hippias, as Master of the Ceremonies, found it harder to get silence for the next turn, and the party began to dissolve into a number of chatting groups.

The livelier groups were those which had managed to add a giggling show girl to their number. Corinna decided that she would be more likely to pick up useful information from those who were talking with grave faces and forgetting even to drink their wine.

Hippias, she noticed, was moving from group to group, speaking to each for several minutes. That was quite correct for a host, but (and here was the strange thing) he never visited any group if it contained a girl. Nor did his expression, as he talked, nor the close attention with which they listened to him, suggest that he was merely making polite conversation.

She came to the conclusion that the real business of the evening was being carried on now, under her very eyes. Hippias was giving out instructions to his fellow plotters.

Somehow she must hear what he was saying. . . . But how? He was extremely wary. For all the wine—and they were drinking it in a strong mixture tonight—there was no drunkenness. There might be laughter and joking, teasing of the show girls and exchanged volleys of raisins or nutshells, but under cover of all that it was a grimly business-like meeting.

Once only was she able to catch a fragment of talk which seemed to mean something.

". . . Hippias will ask him that when they meet."

"Yes, but when will they meet?"

"The night before the Festival. It's too risky for him to come into the city, so Hippias is going out to him."

A third voice cut in. "I'm still not happy about the Council. If they——"

"Don't worry about them! We've got the answer. Hippias told us. In his wife's room!"

There was an outburst of laughter round the table, and even the most intent faces relaxed. Corinna was puzzled.

It did not seem a particular witty remark. Then she remembered: Hippias was not married. She was more puzzled than ever.

She was leaning forward, eager to catch more, when Hippias himself loomed over her, heavy with perfume. She started guiltily. "Ah, the little flute girl! Gorgo's child. So you have honored us at last?"

"Yes," she whispered.

"Good. You played well. Come and sit with me later, and I'll teach you to drink wine. I want to hear what you think about everything. But just now I must see to my guests." He passed on, giving her a familiar slap which did not hurt but brought a flush of fury to her cheeks.

She sat still for a while, more miserable than ever. She had picked up only one piece of information: Hippias was meeting someone, presumably Magnes, outside Athens on the eve of the Festival. It did not seem much of a reward for an evening she had disliked so much. Could she go back and report to Alex, admitting that she had run away before the end? On the other hand, would she find out any more if she stayed until dawn?

Suddenly her eyes brightened as she saw a possible way out. What was the mystery about Hippias' nonexistent wife —or rather, her room? The room itself existed, because the "answer" to something lay there. Perhaps Hippias, as a bachelor, did not use the principal bedroom in the house? Moment by moment Corinna grew more certain. Part of the evidence she was seeking lay in that room upstairs. If she could get it, she would be amply justified in leaving this awful party at once. If Hippias asked for her later, and Mom made a row in the morning, she would have to invent some excuse, that she'd felt sick or something. . . .

The decision made, she waited only for Hippias to turn his back before slipping from the room. The midnight air stung her flushed face, but it was sweet after the heat and scent and fumes of wine. The courtyard was full of slaves, huddled in their cloaks against the cold, waiting with lanterns to escort their masters home. She noted that the big outer door was bolted. It was going to be awkward, slipping away unnoticed.

She took her shoes in her hand and crept upstairs to the family bedrooms and women slaves' quarters. One lamp glimmered on a ledge. It was just enough to light up the doorway of what, from its decoration, must be the principal bedchamber. With thumping heart she grasped the strap of the latch and heard the click within. But the door did not yield. It was locked, and the keyhole was a black, empty slit in the lamplight.

"Hey—what's this?" demanded a rough voice from the stairs.

She turned, panic-stricken. Escape that way was barred. Another staircase mounted into the darkness, and she fled up it. Sandaled footsteps pattered behind her.

She found herself on the roof. Stars blazed overhead, but there was no moon. She was just aware of a pale white shimmer which was the Acropolis, and the dark bulk of the Areopagus hillside rising steeply under the very walls of the house.

"What's the game, eh?" demanded her pursuer. "Thieving, I'll bet! I know you riffraff."

Corinna answered not a syllable. As the slave faced her across the flat roof she retreated into the farther corner, pressing herself back against the parapet. Something tickled her arm and turning, she saw that it was the feathery top of a young cypress which just overtopped the house. She glanced down. Thanks to the tilt of the slope, it was not a very terrifying drop on this side.

She threw flute and shoes over the parapet and launched herself wildly into the arms of the cypress. She lived through a few dreadful moments as the tree bent and

swayed and seemed to fight with her, scratching her, fend-
ing her off. She half fell, half slid, and finally crashed to
the ground, shaken and bleeding. Someone sprang from the
shadows and helped her up.

"Are you all right?" demanded a familiar voice.

"Alex!" she sobbed with relief and delight.

"I've been hanging around all evening," he said hoarsely.
"I hated the idea of your being in there. Look here, if you
are all right, we'd better run."

"Oh, my dress!" she wailed as she groped round for her
shoes, and he knew then that she was all right.

They talked everything over more calmly on the following
morning. Alexis was so busy with final rehearsals that there
was no question of going up to the cave. They met by ar-
rangement on the steps leading up to the Acropolis. There
was a constant stream of people going up and down to the
Parthenon and the other shrines, and no one paid any attention to a boy and girl leaning on the parapet and talking in
low, urgent voices.

"They're planning something, all right," she said. "You
ought to tell someone."

"I know." He clenched his hands. His brows creased
with worry. "Wish I knew how to go about it. Don't you
see? As things stand, it's still such a tall story."

"I like that! You should have been there last night. I
could feel it in the air."

"Yes. . . . But the Council weren't there to feel it, or
the Minister Royal, or even Lucian's uncle! We want evidence if we go to them. What have we got? That strip of
code. We work it out to mean one thing, but suppose they
don't believe us?"

"Anyone who can't see what that code means—once it's
been shown to him—doesn't *want* to see."

"That's just it! Some of the Council may not want to see," he answered grimly.

"Why not?"

"There are five hundred members. Do you really imagine Hippias hasn't got any of his friends planted in a number like that? If our evidence was really strong, the Council would have to act. But if it's doubtful, those fellows will jump up and laugh at it. Try to see it from the Council's point of view," Alexis went on earnestly. "They've got the word of a boy and a girl—and she's not even Athenian. Incidentally, if this business turned out the wrong way, it might be pretty awkward for you and your mother. You might get deported or something."

"I've thought of that," said Corinna more calmly. "That'd be the last straw, of course. Mom's wild enough with me as it is." She pushed back the dark hair which the hilltop breeze was flicking into her eyes. "Heaven knows why I bother about Athens! Whether there's a dictator or a democracy, I'll still be a blessed outcast, pushed down in the gutter."

He ignored the interruption. He was trying to arrange his thoughts as Socrates had taught him to. "What's our evidence beyond that strip of cloth? Just those scraps of talk you overheard last night. No mention of Magnes by name. Magnes has never come into this yet—it's only our guess——"

"You saw him at the torch race! With Hippias!"

"I think I did. I *know* I did. But I can't prove it. It was months and months ago anyhow, and no one believed me then."

"They mentioned the Council last night, anyhow."

"People are always mentioning the Council. How can they help it, if they talk politics? They didn't say anything really suspicious or illegal, like—well, like planning to murder them all, or something like that."

"I wouldn't put it past them. It was very fishy what they said about the room upstairs. And it *was* locked."

"There's nothing fishy about a room being locked. As Hippias isn't married, I don't suppose it's used. I'm seeing it from their viewpoint," Alexis added hastily, noting her impatient pout. "You can bet, too, if there was any question of searching that room, Hippias would get word in time from his friends on the Council. By the time they got the door unlocked, whatever—or whoever—is inside would have been moved out of danger."

"Then I just wasted my time last night!"

"Not at all. You got hold of another piece of information. Hippias is going out to meet someone—Magnes, I bet—the night before the Festival. That's in four days. Nothing drastic will happen before then, obviously. I shall watch out for Hippias that day——"

"And follow him?"

"Yes, and with any luck, I'll see who he meets, and get something absolutely definite to tell the Council."

"I'll come with you——"

"You certainly won't," retorted Alexis firmly. "One shadow's all right—but when a man finds he's got two he begins to wonder! No, seriously, you've done your share, and it's my turn now. I'll get on better alone."

By the evening before the Festival, Alexis was reduced to a state of nervous exhaustion. Or felt he was. For, when the time came for fresh efforts, he found reserves of strength and determination which surprised him.

The dress rehearsal was as painful as such occasions always are. Everything went wrong. Actors flubbed their lines or exchanged what should have been snappy dialogue at a pace more suited to a funeral service. The flute player went temperamental and the dancers tied themselves into hopeless knots. The two men inside the cowskin fell over the edge of the stage through not being able to see properly and, though they luckily injured nothing but their dignity, it took a lot of tact to persuade them to continue. Glaucus got stubborn and demanded last-minute alterations in the long speech which, according to custom, he made direct to the audience in the middle of the play, while the actors were off-stage. Two of the jokes were no longer topical, he complained, and it was absolutely essential that this speech should be up-to-the-minute.

Alexis groaned, pretended to go into conference with Uncle Paintbrush in the back row, and managed to produce six new lines to take the place of the cuts.

The worst of it was, Uncle Paintbrush thoroughly enjoyed the rehearsal and kept declaring it was all splendid. He sat there heaving with amusement, tears streaming down his face, entirely forgetting that he was supposed to have written every word himself. "I only hope the audience will like our piece as much as the author does," said Glaucus waspishly. With the old man so obviously content and blind to every mistake, it was no use Alexis trying to put criticisms into his mouth. It was going to be terrible tomorrow, he thought to himself gloomily, when those empty benches were packed solid with the holiday crowd! Athenian audiences were not kind to failures. He could only pray that they would let poor old Uncle Paintbrush down lightly, and throw nothing heavier than words of insult.

Even a dress rehearsal has to end eventually, especially when there is a rival production waiting for the use of the stage. Early in the afternoon he was able to crawl home and devour the meal he should have eaten at midday.

"I'm spending the night at Uncle's," he told his mother.

"Oh. Is that necessary?"

"Seems sensible. We shall have to get started terribly early. His play might be the first to go on. You never know, there may be last-minute errands to run, crises of one sort or another," said Alexis, with grim memories of the rehearsal. "And he's terribly worked up about the whole thing. I feel I ought to stick around with him till it's all over."

"Oh, do then, darling. It must be a great strain for a man

of his age. But your uncle has obviously got all kinds of qualities none of us ever suspected."

Alexis had already taken the precaution of speaking to his uncle, and fully intended to spend the night at his house—or what was left of the night when he returned from shadowing Hippias. Some sort of alibi was necessary to prevent their worrying at home. It had been awkward enough on the night of the party—after escorting Corinna home he had managed to climb into his own house with the co-operation of young Theo, but the dog had barked and Father had called out, and altogether it had not been an experience he wanted to repeat.

Two other problems had worried him a good deal: how to make sure of not missing Hippias when he started out, and how to avoid being recognized. Luckily, Hippias' door opened upon a busy street, and it was easy to watch it from an archway farther along. He made sure that Hippias was inside the house by asking a slave girl as she hurried forth on an errand, and settled down to wait. To give himself an excuse for squatting under the archway and at the same time a disguise, he had dirtied his face and hands and put on the costume of a peasant boy—a ragged, greasy sheepskin coat, clumsy-looking boots and a brimmed hat, and a shapeless bundle containing nothing in particular. There was something to be said, he reflected with a grin, for being able to raid the theatrical costumes!

So the afternoon passed, and he waited there, watching the doorway with half-closed eyes, the very picture of a tired country lad resting until it was time to start the long tramp back to his village. In case anyone spoke to him he had a wonderful broad dialect rehearsed and ready. He was quite disappointed that he was given no chance to use it.

Foot by foot the last sunshine retreated up the walls, till it gleamed only on the houseroofs and the street grew dim. The sky turned from pale blue and peach to an apple green.

Lights gleamed from upper windows, torches bobbed along the road. Dusk flowed over Athens like an airy, violet sea.

A figure stepped from the house. It was Hippias himself. Two slaves followed him. One carried a torch, both had ironshod staves. They came down the street. Alexis caught a whiff of perfume as Hippias passed within a yard. The slaves clumped after him at a respectful distance. Weariness forgotten, Alexis jumped up, shouldered his bundle, and followed.

For the first two miles there was no difficulty. Plenty of people were moving out through the city gate and along the tree-lined road toward the eastern hills. Hippias kept straight on, as innocently as though bound for a supper party at some neighboring farm. And, among so many other dim figures strung out behind, singly and in groups, an odd peasant boy attracted no notice.

Gradually, however, the stream of people thinned. A huge, lemon-colored moon showed its rim, and then its full disc, above the inky mass of Mount Hymettus. Instead of getting darker, the evening grew light until, as the moon climbed higher and whitened to silver, it was possible to see far more clearly than Alexis liked. He dropped back as far as he dared, and kept within the ebony shadows flung by the cypresses and leafless poplars. The light was so brilliant that he could see the glimmering snows of Hymettus and Pentelicus, riding high in the cloudless heavens above the terraced foothills.

At this point Hippias' slave doused the torch. Alexis heard it die, hissing, in the water of the roadside ditch. The three cloaked figures struck off at an angle across the fields, making toward the Ilissus. The river could be heard quite clearly, its swollen winter flood boiling down in cataracts.

Alexis dumped his burden and followed. It was no longer

needed for disguise and would be only a handicap. Somehow he had to keep up with Hippias without being seen.

"Thought so!" he grunted triumphantly. Trees and rocks had a familiar look. Though this was not the route he usually followed, he knew that the marble quarry was not far away. There had always been a strong possibility that Hippias would meet his mysterious accomplice in the cave where the code message had been found. Now it seemed almost certain.

If I'd only known, he thought to himself! He could have been up there hours ago and fixed himself a hiding place in the inner recesses of the cave. But the thought no sooner occurred to him than he dismissed it. Would the cave have been empty during the afternoon? Whoever had come to meet Hippias might have been waiting there all day; in which case, he could easily have blundered into a trap. He shuddered. With so much at stake, the conspirators would not have been gentle with any spy who fell into their hands.

Now that he knew where the trail was leading him, he was free to take his own line through the undergrowth, using ways he knew from many a daylight exploration. Hippias and his slaves were much less familiar with the lay of the land. There was a good deal of crashing about in front, and the voice of the young aristocrat rose several times in shrill vexation. Stealing carefully through the bushes, Alexis felt that, with so much noise going on, his own movements ran little risk of notice.

When they reached the mouth of the quarry there was a grunted challenge, which Hippias answered.

"So we imagined," said a blunt voice with a Spartan ring. "We've been listening to the racket for the past five minutes."

"Well, good heavens, what does a *little* noise matter up here? We're miles from anywhere."

"We're taking no chances, all the same. Your slaves had

better wait here and help the other men keep watch. Magnes is in the cave. He's been getting some sleep. It was no joke, last night, coming over the hills."

Hippias and the unknown went forward into the quarry. From the whispers in front, Alexis judged that the two slaves were standing with several other men. It was a tremendous stroke of luck that he knew the ground so well. He was able to creep round to the right, outflank the watchers, and slip safely past them into the overgrown quarry. It was mercifully darker there, for the steep cliffs of marble cast the whole area into shadow. It was like a giant bowl of rock, brimming with dark wine.

Firelight gleamed from the cave entrance. He saw two dark shapes silhouetted against it for a few moments as Hippias and his companion scrambled up onto the ledge. A new voice greeted them. He heard Hippias answer, with the same note of respect he had sounded on the night of the torch race, "Sorry you're having to camp out like this, sir! Anyway, you'll sleep in rather more comfort tomorrow night, I can promise you."

"I doubt if any of us will sleep much tomorrow night," Magnes corrected him harshly. "The night *after* that, if all goes well, we should be able to relax."

"Meant that, of course. Silly of me."

"Sit down, then. You have introduced yourself to my very good friend, Callibius, of Sparta?"

"Met down there," said the Spartan briefly.

"Then we can get to business. Callibius, of course, is our link with Sparta. We shall depend a good deal on them— and him. But it will have to be kept in the background. Our freedom-loving countrymen are extremely touchy, Callibius, and they dislike very much feeling dependent in any way on a foreign power!"

"I understand. I've got my orders."

The three men moved back into the cave. The effect was

to deaden their voices so much that Alexis, as long as he remained on the ground below the ledge, could hear only a
dull murmur, competing with the thin cascade which
splashed down the quarry side. If he was to pick up any
more definite information he must risk climbing into a
tree and raising his head high enough to peer over the ledge.
Once more his familiarity helped him. He had scrambled
up by that tree so often that his feet and hands glided
to their usual holds without the need for groping. Not a twig
snapped, not a branch creaked, as he hoisted himself into a
position from which he could see the conspirators seated
around a small fire and catch almost every word they said.

"Yes," Hippias was assuring Magnes, "everything is
fixed for tomorrow night. It's too good a chance to miss."

"I'd rather you'd delayed another month," growled the
Spartan. "Suited *us* better. Still. . . ." He shrugged his
shoulders.

"You see, the Drama Festival gives us such an opening,"
Hippias hurried on persuasively. "You've never seen one of
our festivals, I suppose?"

"No."

"Well, after the plays have finished and it's dark, we have
a grand carnival and a sort of fancy-dress parade—tremendous fun, really—with everyone dressed up in masks
and costumes. Satyrs and bacchants, the nymphs and the
Graces and the Hours, *you* know—" His affected laugh
brayed out, and Alexis saw the Spartan wince. "That's
Magnes' chance to get into the city without being recognized. I thought he might dress up as one of the Hours, it
would make such a good watchword to pass round when
we're ready: 'The Hour has come!' Rather neat, I thought."

Alexis began to wonder why he had ever felt afraid of
Hippias. He had seemed effective enough before. Now,
measured against the grim, calculating Magnes and the dour
Spartan, he shrank in importance. Magnes was a different

proposition. Sitting there with the firelight leaping on his cruel high cheekbones, with that nose and jaw, remorseless as the ram of a war galley, he looked really capable of ruling the city which had cast him out.

"I *have* explained the idea to Callibius," he interrupted quietly, but without rudeness. He puts up with Hippias' silliness, Alexis told himself, because Hippias isn't a fool in every way. In fact, he's extremely useful. And as long as Magnes finds him useful he *will* use him. After that, though, I wouldn't like to be in Hippias' shoes. . . . Magnes must be very clever, as well as bad. He can handle Hippias and his type, he can handle these dumb Spartan officers, and I bet he's got quite another way of handling a citizens' meeting. . . .

The Spartan grunted. "I get it," he agreed. "People will be off their guard tomorrow night because of the carnival. Plenty of drink around and so on."

"And it won't merely help Magnes to come in unrecognized," Hippias went on, undiscouraged. "It'll mean that we can all wear armor under our costumes, ready for when the word's given."

"Now that *is* a help," Callibius agreed, showing his sign of approval at the mention of something military. "But how are you fixed for arms? The first surprise attack, I mean—before you can burst open the armory?"

Hippias laughed again. "I've taken care of that. I have two hundred swords, the same number of shields, fifty spears, a whole lot of long daggers, very handy to carry hidden——"

"Where are they?"

"Safely locked up in the principal bedroom of my house, which has never been used since my parents died!"

Alexis tightened his grip on the slender branches of the tree. So that was the riddle which had so perplexed Corinna! Everything was terrifyingly clear now. Within twenty-four hours there would be blood, as well as wine, running in the streets. . . .

Fascinated, forgetting the strain and weariness of the long day, unconscious of the cramp in the foot he had wedged in the fork of the tree, he strained his ears to catch more details of the plot as Magnes himself began to unfold it.

It was diabolically thorough. Magnes had it all worked out to the last detail.

The chief democratic leaders were to be struck down in the middle of the carnival, but some of the more timid ones were to be left alive on purpose, to be used as tools later.

Rumors were to be circulated to spread panic through the city and to make people think the actual number of the conspirators much greater than it was. So, when the survivors of the Council met hurriedly at dawn, no one would know whom to trust or who was to be the next victim of the assassin's dagger.

With the democrats leaderless, the key points in the city held by rebels, and the population in complete panic, it should be quite easy for one of Magnes' friends on the Council to get up and propose that Magnes be recalled from exile "to save the country." Not many would dare to vote against such a motion— "and any who do," said Magnes, his lip curling, "we shall deal with before they can harm us."

Athens was more than the city itself. Magnes was well aware of that. The frontier garrisons would be surprised and disarmed before they could rally and come to the help of the democracy. As for the troops serving overseas who might cause trouble, "we need only remind them that we hold their families at our mercy," said Magnes, "and that applies not only to the generals and admirals but to any man in the ranks who refuses to toe the line!"

Behind everything, to be called in only if the plotters met

with some serious obstacle, was the armed power of Sparta.

Alexis' blood froze at the efficiency of it all. He must get back to Athens at once, rouse up the Minister Royal himself, and warn him of the peril overhanging the country. If he doubted the story now, let him break into the locked room in Hippias' house and see those stacks of weapons before Hippias could get home and remove them!

He was preparing to get down from the tree when Hippias spoke again. "Just a detail. I want one further name added to the list of those we shall . . . deal with . . . tomorrow night."

"Who?"

"Socrates. He is too dangerous to be left untouched. He is not a man we can bribe or threaten in any way. He'll go on speaking his mind—and asking his questions—and some people will listen to him. We can't afford it at a time like this."

There was a moment's silence while Magnes considered. Then he said, "I quite agree. I can see no way in which I can use Socrates, and he *is* dangerous. I think it's high time he continued his inquiries in another world."

Alexis waited to hear no more. Neatly, without a sound, he let himself down from the tree. And straight into a pair of muscular arms outstretched to receive him.

17

Who is it?" Magnes demanded harshly, peering down from the ledge. "Who've you got there?"

"Shepherd boy, sir, by the looks of it——"

"Let's have a look at him. What were you doing, lad, skulking about at this time of night?"

Alexis ceased to struggle hopelessly against the slave who held his arms twisted behind his back. Thinking quickly, he put on his country accent and whined, "Beg pardon, sir. Didn't mean no harm, sir. Didn't know you was gentlemen, sir—thought you might be thieves, out after the sheep——"

"How did you know anyone was here?"

"Saw the firelight, an'——"

"How long have you been listening here?"

"Only just come, sir, this very minute——"

"That's a lie, sir," broke in the slave. "He was up in the tree before that. That's how we saw him. His head showed against the firelight. He was looking right over the top of the ledge. Must have been there some while, I reckon."

Callibius and Hippias had joined Magnes. The Spartan had plucked a blazing branch from the fire and knelt with it to light up the group of figures below. Hippias exclaimed sharply.

"This isn't a shepherd boy, I know his face! He's Alexis Leonides. Used to hang around Socrates. A fresh, good-for-nothing little——"

Magnes cut him short. His voice was full of quiet menace. "I see. Well, Alexis, who sent you to spy on us?"

"Nobody," said Alexis sullenly, dropping his dialect.

"Do you expect me to believe that? Is it usual for a well-bred Athenian boy to go creeping through the countryside in the dead of night? Why aren't you at home in the city?"

Alexis had a sudden inspiration. "My father's farm is quite near here," he said truthfully. "I often go up there for a night or two. And I *like* wandering about by myself in the dark. It's practice for when I'm called into the army. I don't see why only Spartan boys should go in for stalking and tracking——"

"Do you always dress the part?" Magnes demanded.

"Well . . ." Alexis hesitated. "I didn't want to mess up my best clothes for the Festival tomorrow——"

"He's lying," said Callibius. "He's dangerous. Must have heard all we said. There's only one thing to do——"

"No," said Magnes. "We're not barbarians. We kill when we must, without hesitation. But not wantonly. And a boy. He must be quite good-looking," he chuckled grimly, "with his face washed. Tie his wrists, Cario. Then give him a heave up here."

"Are you going to risk the whole plan——" began the Spartan angrily.

"I'm risking nothing. He'll stay here until it's all over and he can do no harm." He turned to Alexis, who by now had arrived on the ledge, assisted by pushes from below. "Will you be missed tonight?"

Alexis thought it safer to tell the truth. "No, sir."

"That is lucky for you. If your farm people came prowling round with lanterns it would be awkward. We might be compelled to let them find you—with a broken neck. Understand this, Alexis. I will tolerate no interference with my plans. I may not be so lighthearted about shedding Athenian blood as my Spartan friend here is, but if you make any attempt to escape I shall not hesitate for a moment. Is that clear?"

"Yes, sir."

"We shall keep you here tonight and tomorrow. Tie his legs, Cario."

Magnes led the way into the cave. He pointed to the shadowy corner beyond the fire. "Lie down there."

Alexis knelt, awkwardly because of his bound wrists, and flopped over like a sick cow. The slave bound his ankles.

"Behave yourself," said Magnes, "and you will have a share of our food and go home safely when this is over. Play any tricks, though, and I'll hand you over to Callibius. I can't be bothered with ungrateful boys."

The men went back to the entrance, continuing their talk in whispers. After a time Hippias got up, said good night, and left. Callibius and Magnes stretched themselves across the narrow doorway. Even if his hands and legs had been free, Alexis could not have gotten out without disturbing them.

He lay there helpless and hopeless. Toward morning the stuffiness of the cave, added to the exhaustion of the day, overcame even his worry and discomfort. He dropped into a fitful sleep, haunted by dreams in which the Drama Festival and the conspiracy were fantastically mingled. He was acting himself, and the theater was crowded, but somehow it was no longer the theater, but the quarry. He was trying to warn the audience, but he could speak only in verse. He tried to cast his warning into that form—the struggle he had had to rewrite the jokes in Glaucus' speech must still have been fresh in his mind, for when he woke there were half a dozen lines in that meter running through his head, as vivid as though he had composed them in full consciousness:

"Men of Athens, freedom lovers, listen now, be on your guard!
Let the people stand together, and the armory be barred!
On yon hill is perched your peril, long-beaked as a bird of prey—
Masks are not for actors only, traitors keep this holiday!
And at home in Hippias' mansion 'tis no wifely arms that wait—
Cold as iron—comfort only to the traitor at the gate!"

As he struggled back to wakefulness with the verses ringing in his head he heard the herald proclaiming him as victor in the contest. All the theater was crying "Alexis! Alexis!"

He opened his eyes, groaning a little as he became aware of the stiffness in his limbs. "Alexis! Alexis!" It was no dream. His name was really being spoken, but in a breathless whisper, close to his ear.

He should have known Corinna well enough to suspect the meekness with which she had accepted his decision to shadow Hippias alone. She had wasted no time in argument, but had quietly resolved that, when the time came, she would follow behind. If she kept a fair distance behind Alexis he would know nothing—and still less would Hippias—while in an emergency she might be extremely useful.

So it proved. She got as far as the quarry but did not risk trying to pass the men posted there. She was near enough to hear the uproar when Alexis was captured and to gather that he had been taken into the cave, but not to catch any of the conversation afterward. When all was quite again, realizing there was nothing she could do alone, she hitched up her skirt and ran back toward Athens in the moonlight, fleet as the virgin goddess herself, though considerably more bedraggled.

Luckily, the city gates were open. With the Drama Festival beginning soon after sunrise, countrypeople were already trekking in from the villages, ready to camp out in the streets and secure good seats in the theater.

She went straight to Lucian's. Lucian was Alexis' best friend. She could not think of anyone better to go to.

The household was already astir. She pleaded with the slave at the door and soon Lucian appeared, rubbing his eyes. "You?" he said, looking scandalized. "What on earth——"

"I know you don't like me," she said candidly. "That doesn't matter. Alex is in danger." She explained in a whisper. Hippias was plotting with Magnes in the cave. They had caught Alexis listening and taken him inside.

Lucian rose to the occasion splendidly. "I'll tell my father at once. We'll get an armed party together, and——"

"No. That would be terribly dangerous—dangerous to poor Alex, I mean. They might—" she hesitated, shuddering. "They might do something to him. Or use him as a hostage, if they had to fight their way out."

"You're right." Lucian knitted his brows. She felt quite fond of him suddenly. He had gone so pale. He must care a lot about Alexis, after all. "We must think. Can we get him out on our own?"

"I think so." She told him her plan. He stared.

"Do you mean you never even told Alex about it?"

"Never. That first day, of course, I wasn't telling either of you. I didn't know how long we'd stay friends, and I thought a little secret of my own might come in handy later. I suppose it's the way Mom brought me up," she said apologetically. "Not trusting people too much. I meant to tell Alex about it later, but I felt awkward. Didn't like letting him know I'd lied to start with."

Lucian fastened his shoes and they stole away down the street, now gray with the dawn. "Couldn't you have done this on your own, actually?" he asked.

"Not safely. I need someone else to distract their attention."

"Of course, yes . . . I'm glad you came for me, anyhow."

They hurried through the city gate. The sky behind Hymettus was reddening slowly, and the snows were flushed pink.

"Alexis, Alexis!" she hissed in his ear. He stirred, groaning, and saw her beside him in the gloom. "Not a sound," she ordered. "Quick, roll over!"

He turned on his side so that she could saw through the cords which bound his wrists behind him. He could see the jagged cleft of gray sky framed in the cave mouth. The fire had died to a smoldering heap. On the far side of it were scattered cloaks, shoes, and a wine jar. Magnes and Callibius were not visible, but he could hear their voices in urgent consultation just outside.

"I've *done* your ankles," Corinna whispered angrily. "Can't you feel? But I suppose you're too stiff to feel anything much." She gripped his wrist, slipped her other arm round his back, and helped him to struggle upright. "We've got to get out of this, quick."

Only then did he realize the full danger of their position. "How on earth did you slip past them?" he demanded hoarsely. "Now we're both trapped! Listen to them—we haven't a chance——"

"This way," she retorted. She drew him back, farther and farther into the depths of the cave.

"It's no good," he protested. "They'll find us. They'll search till they find us, and then——"

"They won't find us. Keep close behind me. We climb up here. It's a tight squeeze. Watch out for your head."

They were now in darkness and climbing steeply. He was aware of her, hot and panting, somewhere just above him. Then he saw her as a dim shape in a growing twilight. Next time he raised his eyes she was a straining black outline against a circle of blue sky. Soon they were out on the hilltop, with the sea breeze whipping their hair and the mountains standing round them in sunrise glory.

"You never told me about that passage!" he said accusingly. He remembered the day when they had suggested exploring the cave with torches and she had put them off with her talk of falling rock.

"That was my special secret. I wasn't sure I was going to like you—or Lucian. That reminds me, he's down there somewhere." She pointed toward the wooded hillside, falling away below the quarry to where the flooded Ilissus flashed whitely between the trees.

"*Lucian?*"

"Yes, he went smashing about there to attract their attention. We thought it would probably bring them all out of the cave to look. Luckily it did. He'll be all right. They won't catch Lucian."

"No. But we'd better not hang around up here," he said, "or they may find the passage and come climbing after us." He cast a quick glance around, taking in the landmarks.

"I know a different way home, without going near the quarry. We'd better run."

"Of course! Do you know, I'd almost forgotten? The plays will be starting—today's the day!"

"I'm not thinking of that," he said grimly, as they trotted down a goat track into the woods. Then he told her what she had not known before. "Today's fixed for the revolution. We haven't a minute to lose."

18

THE HOUR OF DECISION

The Festival had started when they reached the dressing rooms behind the stage. They could hear the murmur of the audience, swelling and fading like the sea.

The first person they saw was a distracted Uncle Paintbrush. He almost fell on Alexis in his relief. "Thank heaven you've turned up, boy! Luckily we're not on till last——"

"We were afraid something had happened to you," said a level, kindly voice. Alexis was surprised to see Conon, smiling and garlanded. The stern old man had been developing a great interest in the production he was paying for, but he had never given any indication that he would leave his country retreat to see the performance. As though some excuse were needed, he went on, "I felt it was time I broke my rule against theatergoing. I came round to wish you luck." Then, frowning at the boy's appearance, he said, "But why this getup? You're not acting yourself, are you? And

this girl——" He stared at Corinna, and for a moment words
failed him. "Who are you?" he managed to say. "How—
how did you get here?"

"There's no *law* against women in the theater, it's only
silly convention," said Corinna. "And there's a special reason, so you needn't look so shocked——"

"I am not shocked, young lady, but——"

"Please, sir," broke in Alexis impatiently. There were
more important things to discuss than a girl's presence at the
stage door. He must get his news to the authorities, and
Conon was the most reliable grownup within reach. Father,
Lucian's uncle, and everyone else he could think of were
lost somewhere in that multitude in front, and Uncle Paintbrush was useless in a crisis like this. "I must talk to you,
sir. It's terribly important." In an undertone he poured out
his story.

Conon sank onto a stool with an apology. The early start
from home, the unaccustomed crowds, had made him a little
faint. He listened, giving only an occasional nod of under-
standing. Then he rose, gathering his robe about him, his
gaunt face sterner than usual. "This is unspeakable," he
said.

"Whom do we tell, sir—the Minister Royal?"

Conon shook his massive head. "Security comes under
the military committee—ten generals, you know. There's
one on duty every day. I don't know who is in command
today, but it doesn't matter. They're all sitting out there in
the front row, with the other ministers of state."

"Can we get to them?"

"I can. I have a reserved seat quite near—because I'm
backing your uncle's play. Listen," continued Conon deci-
sively. "I'll try to get hold of the general as soon as this first
play finishes. There's a long intermission. I'll ask him to
come around here. Meanwhile," he concluded with a mean-
ingful glance at the boy's sheepskin, "you might find your-

self something more festive to put on. That outfit isn't very respectful to the god, is it?"

He walked away as an outburst of clapping signaled the end of the first comedy. The men dancers broke formation as they passed out of sight of the audience and came swarming into the building. The place was in an uproar, with three sets of principals and three choruses all mixed up together, not to mention three rival authors, their well-wishers, flute players, effects men, and stage mechanics. Conscious that at any moment Conon might return with the commander in chief, Alexis rummaged desperately until he found a reasonably clean tunic in the theater wardrobe, a pair of less boatlike footgear, and a square inch or two of vacant floor space, just inside the door, where he could slip into them and hurl the sheepskin from him forever. It had served its turn.

"You'll need a garland," said Corinna helpfully, sticking her face around the door. "Here you are."

"Where did you get this?"

"I found it," she said demurely. "I don't think I'd better hang around here any longer, I'm getting such black looks."

"Where'll you be?" he said, adjusting the wreath round his temples. "Where can I find you when it's all over?"

"At home. Where else would a nice girl be? Conon called me 'young lady'—did you hear? I think he's a dear. Oh, lord, here he comes again—good-by, Alex, and . . . good luck!"

She slipped away as Alexis stepped out to meet Conon and the military-looking gentleman at his side. It would be impossible to talk inside the building. Between plays it was like a monkeys' fairground.

"This is the boy, General," said Conon. "I can assure you, he's quite a reliable fellow." Alexis squared his shoulders and looked up into the shrewd gray eyes which surveyed him.

"Son of Leon, the athlete, I think?" said the general crisply. "Well, young man, you've done Athens a service. But there's no time to waste." He rapped out half a dozen questions which Alexis answered without hesitation. When it came to a list of the other ringleaders, besides Hippias, the boy could name only a few individuals whom Corinna had noted at the party.

"H'm." The general bit his lip. "There's our one serious difficulty."

"How, sir?"

"Suppose we arrest these few after the performance. What do the rest do? If they feel strong enough, they carry straight on and strike without further delay—that means civil war in Athens tonight, my boy, and even though we'll win, thanks to your warning, it's a nasty thing to face."

"Perhaps they wouldn't dare," said Alexis hopefully.

"In that case they'd go underground—and we might not be able to find out who they were. That means no civil war tonight, but civil war in six months, a year, whenever they feel ready for another go. See what I mean, boy? If only we could make a clean sweep of the whole gang now!"

"You need some sort of trick," suggested Conon, "that would make them show their true colors. I remember an old story, about a king who suspected some of his courtiers but didn't know who the traitors were. He had a man rush in and shout 'Everything's discovered!' and then he saw by their faces——"

"Yes, yes, I remember," said the general with an impatient laugh, "but you're not suggesting that someone should leap up in the theater and shout that? That's where Hippias and his friends are at this moment—I've seen *him* with my own eyes, as it happens. But we can't study the faces of thousands——"

"Of course not, General. I didn't mean the *same sort* of

trick. I confess I can't think of anything that would suit these circumstances."

"I can!" cried Alexis in a sudden flash of inspiration. "If Hippias is sitting in the audience, he can't possibly know that I've escaped. Magnes may have sent someone down to warn him, but he'd never find him in that crowd— he'd have to wait till the plays finish. But suppose Hippias *did* get a warning that the plot was discovered, would he go on sitting there, enjoying the play?"

"I doubt it," said the general dryly. "I fancy he'd waste no time in starting for the frontier!"

"And wouldn't every other conspirator do the same— especially if he saw Hippias pushing out of the theater?"

"Certainly. Rats leave a sinking ship together. But how can it be done? We don't want a riot in the theater. Re. member, it's a religious festival."

"We can give that warning, sir, so that every conspirator gets it at the same moment—but nobody else will notice a thing, except you and the other generals!"

"How do you mean, boy?"

Alexis' eyes were shining. "From the stage, sir! *You* get soldiers posted at the exits and grab every man who walks out in the middle of my play. *I'll* write a new piece that'll send every plotter scuttling for the frontier!"

Glaucus grumbled when told to learn six new lines at the last moment, but a few curt words from the general brought him in line. He was to speak whatever the boy Alexis ordered, without altering a syllable. The new lines were to remain a secret until they were spoken from the stage.

"Don't let anyone hear you mumbling them beforehand," said the general. "Don't discuss 'em, don't even think about 'em. Just say them when the moment comes—and loud enough for everyone to hear. This is a matter of life and death. If it goes wrong through any fault of yours, you'll face a charge of high treason—I'll promise you that," he concluded ferociously.

It was lucky, Alexis reflected, that Glaucus was an experienced chorus leader. Some actors would have been paralyzed with fright by the general's dark threats. But Glaucus' professional pride was stung, and he replied, with some dignity, that he could surely be relied upon to speak any lines given him with the utmost discretion and clarity.

"You'd better," said the general. "Well, my boy," he told Alexis, "you've spoiled *my* theatergoing for the day! Pity. I was getting curious to see the last item on the program—can't quite make out who *is* the author!"

He went off to make arrangements. Troops must be paraded to guard the exits, close the city gates, defend all key positions, and raid the arms dump at Hippias' house. The second play had started. He had barely a couple of hours for everything.

Meanwhile Alexis scribbled furiously. Strange how vividly he remembered those lines from his dream! They were not brilliant, but they would do. Every conspirator would understand them, recognize the distinctive nose of Magnes in the "long-beaked bird of prey," and realize that the plot was discovered in all its details—the seizing of the armory, the use of carnival disguise, and the arms dump. The mind did queer things in sleep. Perhaps Plato was not completely crazy when he used to talk about the spirit wandering off into strange dreamworlds?

"There you are, Glaucus," he said, handing over the lines. "Don't let anyone else see them—you know what the general said."

"I do," said the chorus leader gloomily.

Then it was the intermission again, and at last the moment he had often imagined. A hush fell over the audience as the herald rose in his place to announce the final play. In a voice which rang round the crowded hillside he declaimed the usual formula:

"Alexis, son of Leon, presents his comedy—"

Alexis the younger was probably the only person who did not thoroughly enjoy the first half of *The Gadfly*. Looking back on it later, he scarcely remembered it. He was too keyed up, waiting for that vital moment in the middle when, the characters having retired and left an empty stage, Glaucus would step forward from the chorus and address the audience. Until then he was impatient of everything—even the long waves of laughter which greeted his own jokes and rolled round the theater, holding up the action.

To see better, and to escape from poor Uncle Paintbrush's nervous babbling, he climbed to the roof of the dressing room, to the dizzy point where actors appeared when they were supposed to be gods speaking from heaven. Crouching so as not to be seen, he peered down. The narrow strip of the stage itself was almost hidden, so that he could not see the principals, though their resonant voices came up to him distinct as bells. Farther out, the big circular dancing place was clearly visible, with Glaucus and his chorus grouped, now still as statues, now moving in and out, weaving their intricate patterns. Beyond them again was the front row of armchairs, with the priest of Dionysus in the central place of honor, and the ministers and officials ranged on either side. One seat was vacant, that of today's commander in chief. Behind and above, mounting to the calm spring sky and the resplendent temples of the Acropolis, was the audience in its thousands, brown-faced, garlanded, rainbow-gay in holiday garb.

Somewhere, scattered among those close-packed rows, were Hippias and his fellow traitors. . . . Alexis dug his nails into his palms. The suspense was unbearable.

Now! Glaucus was moving out, grotesque in his comic mask and striped tights. The audience sat back, ready to be amused. This was the traditional moment when the author wrote as himself, not as one of his characters. One by one the topical references went home. The crowd shook like a cornfield rippling in the wind. A reference to Socrates brought a roar of good-humored, affectionate laughter. Good old Socrates! No harm in him, really. . . . More use to Athens than plenty of other people we could name. . . .

Glaucus spoke more seriously now. He had a magnificent voice. It rang out, filling the bowl of the theater, reaching to the last row of spectators standing on the skyline. He warned the audience of dangers threatening Athens far more serious than the teaching of a philosopher. There was absolute stillness as he worked up to the climax:

*"Men of Athens, freedom lovers, listen now, be on your
    guard!*
Let the people stand together, and the armory be barred!
*On yon hill is perched your peril, long-beaked as a bird of
    prey—*
Masks are not for actors only, traitors keep this holiday!
*And at home in Hippias' mansion 't is no wifely arms that
    wait,*
Cold as iron—comfort only to the traitor at the gate!"

He stepped back into the ranks of the chorus. There was a round of applause, but with a certain hesitation about it. A murmur of question and comment ran along the benches, to be hushed as the principals came out onto the stage again, and the comic cow made its first triumphant entrance, reducing the audience to delirious laughter.

There were some spectators, however, who had not been in the least puzzled by those concluding lines. They did not stay to be amused by the antics of the cow.

From his lofty viewpoint Alexis saw figures start up, some singly, some in twos and threes, and push their way roughly toward the exits. There was a good deal of indignation among the people they disturbed, and for a few moments the tension of the play sagged as they muttered and grumbled and shouted "Sit down!" But the cow won another tumultuous round of clapping with some ridiculous prank which Alexis could not see, and at once the play regained its hold. The inexplicable, ill-mannered departure of the few was forgotten, and everyone else settled down to enjoy the second half of the play.

This time the young author was among them. The trick had worked. Athens was safe.

When Lucian clambered up to find him on the roof, he had to prod Alexis twice before getting any response. Alexis turned furiously, but the protest died on his lips when he saw who it was and remembered what he owed to Lucian.

"Thanks for this morning!" he hissed.

"It's all right. It was fun. I led them a merry chase, in and out of the river. Say, Alex—they've got troops all round the theater!"

"I know. Tell you later. Look," Alexis begged in a hoarse whisper, with the frankness only possible between bosom friends, "would you mind shutting up just till this is over? I want to listen to my play."

"*Your* play—" began Lucian with a stupefied expression. But Alexis had already turned his head and was peering down into the sun-drenched dancing place where the chorus, like vivid insects, had resumed their patterned dance. Lucian did not trouble to ask his question again. The rapt look on his friend's face gave him the answer. Proud and excited, Lucian dropped on his knees beside him, and there they crouched together, hardly moving a muscle until the play was over.

So old Alex had really written this! The backchat which rocked all those thousands out in front, the lyric choruses which held them in a breathless hush. . . . A lump grew in his throat as the last chorus swelled to its triumphant climax—that chorus into which Alexis had packed all he felt and thought about Athens, which was to be sung in later years by Athenians all over the world:

> "Violet the crown of our city,
> And sea-green the hem of her robe!"

When the last words had died away and the plaintive echoes of the flute accompaniment had faded, the audience paid it the supreme compliment—a few moments of enchanted silence, then a great intake of breath and a storm of clapping, stamping, and shouting which made the hollowed hillside echo like a drum. Lucian stole a glance at Alexis, uncomfortably aware that his own eyes were wet. But the extraordinary thing was—so were the eyes of Alexis, though he had written the blessed thing!

Very little was said while the ten judges were casting their votes. The crowd hummed and babbled, restless as the sea, but the two boys on the roof were silent, exhausted by the events of the past few hours. Lucian sat up at length. "Here we go," he said. And from below them rang out the voice of the herald:

"The prize for the best play is awarded to *The Gadfly* of Alexis, son of Leon. . . ."

19

Conon insisted on giving a grand party to celebrate the victory of *The Gadfly*—"and any other cause for rejoicing which may occur to us," he added with a twinkle in his stern eye, though (as Alexis pointed out afterward) he could not have known, when he said that, just how many other causes for rejoicing there would be.

"I'm afraid I haven't made any definite preparations," he confessed. "Of course, I knew that the backer of the winning play was expected to entertain the cast afterward, but to be quite honest, I never thought we had a chance against Aristophanes! Still, we can soon fix things up. A friend has promised me the use of his town house. The question is, can we get a cook?"

"I think I could find you one, sir," Alexis volunteered.

"I'm quite sure you could!" said Conon, almost jovially. "Now that I know you wrote your uncle's play *and* exposed the Magnes plot, I should be very disappointed if you couldn't do a little thing like finding me a cook."

183

"Well, I had a lot of help from Corinna, you know——"

"That striking-looking child I saw at the stage door?"

"Yes, sir. And actually I'll have to get her help once more. Her mother's the cook I am after!"

"Get her, then, my boy. Ask her to plan for fifty. There's the full cast, nearly thirty, and your family, and your young friend Lucian here, and—anybody else *you'd* like to ask?"

Alexis hesitated. Then he plunged. "Would you mind very much, sir, if we invited—Socrates?"

"By all means, if he'll come. Tell my slave where to find him."

"We can probably catch him at his house, sir. You see," said Alexis, remembering wistfully that *The Gadfly* had been written for Socrates, "he almost never goes to the theater, so I don't suppose he has seen the play. And as there'd be none of his usual friends about in the streets, he'd probably stay at home till it was all over and there was somebody to talk to again."

"Then he can talk to me over dinner tonight," said Conon briskly. "Tell my slave where he lives, and get along to this cook of yours—what's her name?"

"Gorgo, sir."

"Gorgo?" Conon echoed the name in a puzzled tone. "I've heard that name before."

"I guess you have, sir, she's one of the best in Athens. But I think she's free tonight, because she's not very well known in Athens yet—they've only moved here recently from Syracuse——"

"Then how have I heard of her?" Conon muttered. "I haven't been to a party for years. She was that girl's mother, you said? H'm, never mind, never mind." He turned to his slave. "When you have delivered the invitation to Socrates, run home as fast as you can and ask your mistress to dress and come to the party. Tell her it'll be a quiet affair and the ladies can keep to themselves if they're shy. I know it's not usual, but, hang it, it *is* carnival night. There'll be no heavy drinking, tell her, no flute girls or anything of that sort——"

"Excuse me, sir," Alexis interrupted, the corners of his mouth twitching, "we must have one flute girl or the cook won't come—and, with all due respect, sir, neither will I!"

Conon stared aghast. "You don't mean to tell me that girl's a flute player——"

"Not in the ordinary way, sir—but this isn't going to be an ordinary party, is it?"

Nor was it.

The first sight which greeted Alexis' eyes when he passed through the archway of the inn was a moth-eaten sheepskin coat, a pair of battered shoes, and a broadbrimmed peasant's hat, tumbled in a heap on the ground.

Corinna rushed out of the kitchen to greet him. "Oh, Alex, congratulations!" she cried.

"You've heard, then?" he said, vexed. He had run all the way after leaving Conon, hoping to be first with the news of his victory.

"*Heard?*" She flung up her head and laughed her silent laugh. "Do you think I'd have missed seeing as well?" She pointed to the garments on the ground. "You can have your smelly old sheepskin back. It was very useful in the theater—the men both sides of me edged away as far as they could!"

"You mean—" he began delightedly. "Well, you *are* a little——"

"Now then!" said Gorgo, bustling out of her kitchen. "What's come over you two? Never in all my born days——"

"I've brought you a commission," Alexis explained. "Tonight. Dinner for fifty. Best of everything. No expense spared. You will, won't you?"

Gorgo's face creased with professional pleasure. "You bet I will, Master Alex! I always said you were a good friend to us. Best of everything it shall be!"

Alexis ranked that evening as one of the happiest in all his life.

There was the wonderful moment when Father arrived, and hugged him, and then stood back at arm's length and stared at him with a kind of awe. "And it's really true, what they're saying all over the city? That you wrote the play yourself, and not Uncle Alexis at all? My boy, I'm proud of you!" That was before Father even knew about the part he had played in exposing the conspiracy.

Then there was Mother, rather timid at coming out to a party, and reassured only by the promise that she could sit with Demetria and peep at the festivities from another room. "I wasn't at all surprised, darling," she whispered as she kissed him. "I always knew there was more in you than your father realized." Which made him smile, because she had said much the same about Uncle Paintbrush, but then, dear Mother always thought the best of everyone!

Philip, home on leave this time, added shy big-brotherly congratulations, and Theo made a solemn little speech till Alexis tweaked his ear to stop him. Nico vowed that, if only she had known, she too would have dressed up as a boy and gone to the theater. Uncle Paintbrush, in his thoroughly unselfish way, enjoyed the party almost more than anybody—it was such a relief, he said, to give up pretending to be clever, and he was looking forward to a quiet day at the pottery once more.

Socrates was a great success. He got on extremely well with Father, whose views, like a great many other people's, had been mellowed by *The Gadfly*. It was Theo, however, who fastened on the old philosopher like a limpet, and the pair of them sat in a quiet corner wagging their heads and heedless of everybody else until just after midnight, when Theo went to sleep in the middle of a sentence. Socrates smiled, laid him gently back on a cushion, and moved over to cross-examine Glaucus on the Nature of Rhythm.

But the great moment came earlier, just after the meal, when Corinna entered, flute in hand. She looked very grown-up that night in a long dress of some shimmering blue-gray stuff to match her eyes. She wore no ornament but an old silver brooch in the shape of a grasshopper. She had had it ever since she could remember, and wore it only on special occasions, to bring her luck.

As she played, Conon walked quietly through the doorway into the adjoining room, where his wife and Alexis' mother and one or two other ladies (including a somewhat rebellious Nico) were sitting at a respectable distance from the main festivities. Demetria looked up and smiled. After so many quiet years in the country, she was enjoying this glimpse of life.

"What a pretty girl!" she whispered.

Conon gave her a strange glance. "Does she remind you of anyone, my dear?" he said casually.

Demetria bent forward and peered through the doorway. She shook her head. "I can't remember."

"That is hardly surprising. It was . . . some time ago. And you never saw the other girl properly. Only her reflection in your mirror."

Demetria stared up at him with knitted brows. "What do you mean, Conon?"

"She is the image of yourself at that age. It struck me the moment I saw her this morning."

Demetria gave a little laugh, modest but pleased. "I was never as pretty as that. I suppose there *is* some resemblance, but it's hard to see these things when it's yourself."

"The absolute image," Conon persisted.

"But what a coincidence!"

"So I thought, till I asked her mother's name. It's Gorgo."

"No." Demetria took in her breath sharply. She went pale and clutched at her heart. Alexis thought she had been taken ill and sprang through the doorway to help, but she recovered herself. "If it is," she whispered hoarsely, "There is nothing we can do. We have no right. We did wrong, and we must pay for it. She is happy as she is."

"She *is* not," Conon retorted. "Nor is Gorgo. They are fond enough of each other in a way, but the child is quite unfitted for this life. Gorgo admits that."

"You've spoken to her?"

"Yes. She's here now—in the kitchen."

"No, the girl—what do they call her—Corinna?"

"Not yet. I had to break it to you first."

"Bring her now, Conon, oh, bring her now!" And as Corinna, her tune finished, came wondering through the doorway, Demetria exclaimed, low under her breath, "Look, she still has my brooch—the silver grasshopper!"

Corinna stood pale and silent while Conon and Demetria explained, interrupting each other frequently, Conon to insist that it had been all his fault, and Demetria declaring that she was equally to blame.

As Uncle Paintbrush had told Alexis before, Conon and Demetria had married for love, in defiance of their families. It had begun as a boy-and-girl affair, and Demetria had refused all other suitors until Conon was able to marry her. For years they had no child, and they had given up hope when at last a baby was born—not the son and heir Conon so passionately wanted in those days, but a girl. The chance of a boy coming later seemed remote, and so it proved. There was only one thing to do, a thing by no means unheard-of in well-to-do families: to make an exchange with some woman willing, for a consideration, to accept a newborn girl in place of her boy. They had found Gorgo ready enough. She needed money, she was leaving Athens for one of the colonies, and she felt that a daughter would be much more use to her in afteryears.

"Your mother was always against the idea," Conon insisted firmly. "You must never hold it against her. It was my decision. I only realized later how nearly I had broken her heart. Can you forgive *me*? You have nothing to forgive her."

Corinna looked up into his gaunt, timeworn face. She remembered all Alexis had told her about him. She thought of the little tomb under the trees—how strange, that must really be Gorgo's boy who lay there! But Conon had loved him, and he had died. If Conon had done wrong in sending his own daughter away, he had paid for it in the sorrow of these later years.

So that was what Gorgo must have been thinking of tonight in the kitchen, when she had suddenly clutched her, given her a smacking kiss, and said: "You'll never settle for this life, dear, I can see that. You'll have to get right out of it all. I only want you to be happy. But we'll always be good friends, won't we?"

Gorgo knew then. It was going to be all right. Corinna reached up and kissed her father, and then flung herself into Demetria's arms. . . .

Hours later, when everything had been explained to everybody, and the party was beginning to break up in the dawnlight, Alexis and Corinna stood in the street, drinking in the fresh cold air. "So you're going to be an Athenian lady after all!" he teased her. "How are you going to like that?"

"It won't be so bad!" she retorted. "Don't think I'm becoming all prim and proper overnight. We shall be living out on the farm, and a girl's much freer in the country. You needn't think I shall vanish upstairs every time you call!"

"How do you know I'll call? It's a long walk."

She pouted and said nothing to that. For a few moments they stood silent in the street. Cocks were beginning to crow. The last revelers were tottering home in their bedraggled costumes. The sky lit suddenly with the glory of sunrise, and framed in the gap at the end of the street, riding aloft over the white houses, they saw the Acropolis hill, mauve-shadowed, the city's crown of violet.

Corinna slipped an arm through his. "You know, Alex," she murmured, "it *is* wonderful—in all kinds of ways—knowing that I'm an Athenian!"

For the information of those interested in history, this story is laid in the period just before 400 B.C., when the Athenian democracy was nearing the end of its tragic struggle with Sparta. Socrates, Plato, and Xenophon are, of course, world-famous figures, but our Alexis can hardly be the same as the writer of lost comedies who occurs in the records of Greek literature, because his dates are wrong.

The lines from Euripides, in Chapter Two, are quoted by kind permission from the translation of his *Trojan Women* by Professor Gilbert Murray, O.M., D.C.L., which is published by the Oxford University Press.